BETWEEN A ROCK
AND A HARD PLACE

Also by Alden R. Carter:

Growing Season

Wart, Son of Toad

Sheila's Dying

Up Country

Dancing on Dark Water
(originally published as *RoboDad*)

Dogwolf

BETWEEN A ROCK
AND A HARD PLACE

ALDEN R. CARTER

SCHOLASTIC INC.
New York Toronto London Auckland Sydney
Mexico City New Delhi Hong Kong

ISBN 0-590-48685-3

Copyright © 1995 by Alden R. Carter.
All rights reserved. Published by Scholastic Inc.

SCHOLASTIC and associated logos are trademarks and/or registered trademarks of Scholastic Inc.

12 11 10 9 8 7 6 5 4 3 2 1   8 9/9 0 1 2 3/0

Printed in the U.S.A.   01

First Scholastic printing, September 1998

For
Bill and Rita Dietsche

Acknowledgments

Many thanks to all who helped with *Between a Rock and a Hard Place*, particularly my editor, Regina Griffin; her assistant Kim Stitzel; my mother, Hilda Carter Fletcher; my friends Dave and Pauline Samter, Laurie Meyer, Dean Markwardt, and Steve Sanders; and my in-laws and canoeing companions Dave, Terry, Melody, Wendi, Dan, and especially Dale Shadis. As always, I owe the greatest debt to my wife, Carol.

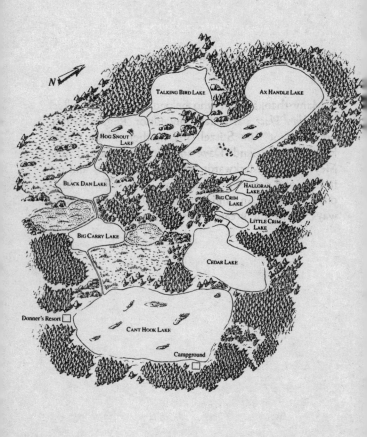

CHAPTER ONE

Dad folded the map. "So, there you have it. An easy two days from Cant Hook to Ax Handle, three or four days fishing, and two or three days back. Just a paddle in the park. Any questions?"

I glanced at Randy, but he was gazing off across the lake toward the last glimmer of the sunset. I shrugged. "I think we've got it, Dad."

"So, you fired up?"

I scratched a mosquito bite. "Yeah, sure, Dad." He frowned, and I managed a smile. "Uh, just want to get at it, that's all."

He grinned. "Well, you guys are going to have one heck of a fine time. Believe me. Our dad did in the thirties, we did in the sixties, and your brother and his buddy Pete did four or five years ago."

"More like six," I said.

He calculated. "Yeah, I guess it was that long ago. Hardly seems possible. Well, anyway, we all had a great time. Isn't that right, bro?"

Bro? I thought. Come on, Dad.

Uncle Jerry looked up from where he was messing

1

with our packs on the far side of the campfire. "You bet, big brother. I'd trade a lot to be fifteen and doing it again."

Well, don't let a few decades stop you, I thought. Shove off in the morning. Randy and I'll be just fine hanging out at that cushy resort, drinking your beer, and rodding around ol' Cant Hook in your motorboat. Go have a blast.

The old guys, as Randy called them, did another God-what-a-great-time-we-had anecdote for us — this one about catching a giant fish of some kind and then nearly losing it. As usual, Uncle Jerry took the lead with his salesman's gift for bull, while Dad — always the engineer — corrected the details. Randy ignored them, I suffered through.

When Dad got up to get another beer and Uncle Jerry went back to messing with our packs, I thought of trying to escape to the lake. I'd walk along the rocky beach to see what kind of yellow the firelight threw on the dark water. Not that I tried to paint such things anymore, I was just curious. But before I could gather the energy, Dad was back and ready to deliver standard lecture number twenty-eight. (Or maybe it was number twenty-nine; it was hard to keep track after a while.)

He opened his Pabst, worked his butt around on the log to get comfortable, and shifted into his pep-talk mode. "Now, listen, boys. Hit the portages like you're marines. If you stand around worrying about how tough it's going to be, you'll be discouraged before you even start. Just hit the beach, throw the packs on your backs, and get moving. If you can, try to carry everything in one trip. Otherwise, you'll have to hang the food pack

2

out of reach of bears before going back for the canoe. More work, more mosquito bites, less time fishing."

Uncle Jerry nudged Randy. "You getting this, Charlie?"

Randy mumbled, "Sure, Dad," and started digging around in his leather satchel. His hand came out with the spring-loaded-needle gizmo he uses to jab himself in the finger whenever he gets bored or decides it's time to check his blood.

Dad hesitated and then went on. "Now, the bears aren't really dangerous. They aren't grizzlies, just your ordinary, everyday black bears. But if one of them gets hold of your food pack, you'll have one sweet hell of a time getting it back. So, don't give 'em a chance. Hang it up every night and every time you're going to be away from it for even a few minutes."

Uncle Jerry looked at me. "Now, Mark, as I told you yesterday, Charlie here needs his chow. If — "

Randy snapped, "Dad, I'm the diabetic, remember? I don't need a damned nursemaid. I've been handling the Big D on my own for a long time."

Uncle Jerry held up his palms, laughing. "Don't take my head off, son. I know you have, and you do a fine job, too. I just want Mark to understand."

"He knows all he needs to know. Now just drop it. And quit with the Charlie crap while you're at it." He zapped the needle into the ball of a finger without even wincing. Uncle Jerry winked at me and went back to poking around in the food pack.

Dad cleared his throat. "Let me see your compass, Mark." I reached under my sweatshirt for it, pulled the cord over my head, and handed it to him. He set it beside his on the log and waited for the needles to steady. "It's dead on," he said, handing it back. "Just don't lose it. I'd hate to give up some good fishing looking for you guys." He reached for the map. "Which means maybe we ought to have one more look at the chart."

God, not again. "Dad, we've got it. Okay?"

He laughed. "Well, maybe in the morning, then. You about ready to hang those packs, Jerry?"

"Just about. Let me get the rope straightened out."

"Come on, Mark," Dad said. "Mr. Bruin could be wandering around here just as easily as anywhere else, and I'd like to get a good night's sleep."

We lugged the big Duluth packs to the far side of the clearing, where Uncle Jerry had slung a rope over a sapling the Park Service had left lashed between two trees. "You probably won't have a ready-made setup at every campsite," Dad said. "So one of you might have to shinny some." I nodded. He looped the end of the rope through the straps of the lighter pack and snapped the hook over the line. With a grunt, he lifted the pack over his head.

Uncle Jerry pulled it into position so it swung high above our heads. He tied off the rope with a few expert flicks of the wrist and then flipped a second rope neatly over the sapling. I caught the end and — very conscious of Dad watching critically — attached the bigger pack. "Ready," I called, and strained to hoist it, feeling the weight come off as Dad got his hands underneath. We pushed it as high as we could while Uncle Jerry heaved on the rope. Randy sauntered over to give him a hand tying it off. Nice you could join us, I thought.

"Is all this really necessary?" Randy asked when we'd stepped back to catch our breath. "What if we just put the packs under the canoe?"

I groaned. God, don't ask them stuff like that, we'll get the whole speech again. And, of course, we did. While Dad and Uncle Jerry started batting bear stories back and forth, I glared at Randy. But he only shrugged and wandered off toward the shore, leaving me to deal with the old guys. Thanks heaps, Charlie.

Back when we were kids, I'd known Randy better, even liked him when we'd played together at family reunions in Minneapolis or St. Louis or at Grandpa's home in Winona. But that was a long way back, and I hadn't seen much of him in the years since Grandpa died and everybody else got too busy for reunions. Now I barely knew him and what I did know I didn't much like.

After Randy and Uncle Jerry went to bed, I stood with Dad on the shore of the bay under an immense, lonely sky filled with more stars than you can ever imagine in the city. Dad got a cigar going, about his third of the evening. I hadn't seen him smoke in a couple of years, but he was letting go now that he was in the North and away from Mom and the twins. I fidgeted, trying to get up the nerve to tell him what I'd been hinting at for weeks: I thought this trip was going to be a bummer. A big one. He sighed, sounding more self-satisfied than sad. "God, I envy you, son.

You are going to have a time you'll remember the rest of your life. I wish we could go with you."

"Well, you could, Dad. I mean — "

He shook his head. "No, this is something you guys need to do on your own. You don't need a couple of old farts like Jerry and me messing it up for you. And if your big brother wanted to go along, I'd tell him the same thing. He had his trip, now it's your turn."

Brother Bob. I remembered the pictures he'd brought back from the Boundary Waters all those years ago. I'd dreamed then of going on the same trip someday. But that was back when I wanted to do everything my big brother did, and I'd grown out of that a long time ago. This fall he'd be a senior in electrical engineering at CalTech and cadet commander of the Army ROTC unit — two things I'd never be or want to be. And if my attitude happened to disappoint a few people — my parents, Bob, and about three dozen teachers who'd known us both — I didn't give a major damn. Or a minor one. Screw 'em.

Dad was going on. "I know you're a little anxious, son. But we've taught you just about everything we know in the last couple of days. You both know how to paddle a canoe and you both know how to swim. Keep your heads on straight, always know where you are, portage any rapids, be careful of fire, and — "

"Always hang the food pack," I finished for him.

He laughed. "See? You've got all the important stuff down. Nothing to worry about."

"How do you know Randy can swim? It's been too cold to swim."

"Randy could swim like a fish when he was just a

little boy. Don't you remember how he used to swim out to the raft with Bob and your aunt at that resort near your grandpa's?"

Oh, I remembered that. Randy, Bob, and Aunt Marlene swimming out to the raft, leaving me standing in water up to my waist, too afraid to go any deeper. "Yeah, but that was before he got this — "

"His illness doesn't have a thing to do with how well he can swim. And don't start giving me any grief about your swimming. You can swim just fine. Bob took care of that years ago."

Yeah, Bob'd taken care of that, all right: *Swim or drown, punk, because I don't give a major rip either way.* "Yeah, hooray for Bob," I muttered.

He made like he hadn't heard, as he spent a moment relighting his stogie. He shook out the match and exhaled a cloud of blue smoke that billowed briefly against the stars before dissolving in the night breeze that had begun rippling the water of the lake and the branches of the pine along the shore. "Now don't get spooked by how big and lonely this country can seem," he said. "There's more danger crossing the street in Minneapolis than you'll find up here."

"I haven't seen any bears in Minneapolis."

He chuckled. "No, but we've got plenty of street people. Give me the bears; they never carry knives."

"Yeah. But, Dad, I really worry about Randy — "

"Oh, don't worry about him. He's been treating himself for years."

"Maybe, but he doesn't seem very enthusiastic about this trip."

"That's just Randy for you. You're both a little jumpy.

7

Your brother and Pete were, too. Now there was a kid born a couple of centuries too late. Do you remember Pete?"

How could anyone forget Pete the Mountain Man? Even more than Bob, Pete had been my hero. Still was in a funny sort of way. "Yeah," I said, "he went to school out west to become a forest ranger."

"Yep. Last time I talked to his mom, she told me he's got a job lined up in one of the national forests in Montana. I think she said Flathead or maybe it was Bitterroot." He frowned, the engineer in him unhappy with forgetting a detail. "Anyway," he said, "Bob and Pete made this trip, and you can do it, too."

"We're not Bob and Pete."

He sighed, trying to keep the irritation out of his voice. "No, you're not. You're Mark and Randy, and you can do just as good a job and have just as good a time if you want to."

I felt like saying: Yeah, but suppose I don't want to go on this stupid trip at all? I've got nothing I want to prove and I am *not* going to have a good time because I don't like bugs, I don't like Randy, and I sure as hell don't like water. But I only stared at the ground and mumbled, "I guess."

He smiled. "Relax, you'll both do fine. Just remember that you're in charge. Don't boss Randy around or anything, but I'm depending on you to make the right decisions. You're the one who's spent time in the woods."

Time in the woods? He had to be kidding. Sure, I'd been a Boy Scout for a couple of years — hikes, weekend camping trips, and all that. But *this* was a damned sight different. For the next eight or nine days, Randy and I were supposed to paddle through the Minnesota wilderness, following a wide arc that would take us across ten lakes before we met up with the old guys again at the opposite end of Cant Hook. And all because our granddad had started some big coming-of-age tradition for Severson men some sixty years ago. Well, horseshit. All the coming-of-age I wanted this summer involved trying to get very friendly with a certain Ms. Sonia Long somewhere within the city limits of Minneapolis. Damn. If I lost my chance with her just because of this stupid trip —

"Well, we'd better turn in," Dad said. He took a final drag on his cigar and flipped it into the coals of the dying fire. He slapped me on the shoulder. "Tomorrow is going to be one big and very fine day."

I nodded, trying not to look queasy. Maybe it'd rain like hell. Or better yet, snow. But they'd probably make us go anyway. No wimps among the Severson men. Or at least none who'd admit it.

Randy was sprawled out in his sleeping bag, his legs draped over my air mattress. I shoved them over to his side of the tent, and he grunted. I pulled off my boots, jeans, and sweatshirt, swearing under my breath at the cramped quarters, and wrestled my way into my sleeping bag. "You zip the fly?" he asked sleepily.

"Yeah, I zipped the fly. What do you take me for?"

"Just asked. You don't have to get grouchy."

"Well, it was a stupid question." He grunted again

and turned over. I lay on my back for a few minutes, staring at the dim glow of the campfire reflecting on the roof of the tent. "You still awake?" I asked.

"What do you think? Are you about done thrashing around, or should I give you another hour?"

I bit back a sarcastic reply about spending half the last two nights trying to keep his big feet off my air mattress. "So, what do you really think of this trip?" I asked.

"I think it's a crock. But there's no way out of it, so I figure I'll just live through it."

"What'd your mom think?"

"*The Mom*? Shit. I rang her pager a couple of times, but she never got back to me. She's too busy being St. Louis's up-and-coming woman lawyer to worry about stuff like this. Marcia and I don't see her more than an hour every other day or so." He turned over again and worked his shoulders around trying to get comfortable. "How come I always have to sleep on the side with the big rocks?"

"You don't. The really big ones are over here."

"Yeah, I'll bet. So, what'd your mom say?"

I shrugged. "Back in the spring she bitched a little after supper one night about me being too young, but Dad reminded her that Bob was only fifteen when he went with his buddy, the Mountain Man. Then the twins got into a fight, and she went to deal with that."

"Who's the Mountain Man?"

"A guy named Pete Miller. He wanted to be some kind of mountain man or trapper or something. I'll tell you about him sometime. Anyway, she brought it up a couple more times, but about July she started siding with Dad. After that, I couldn't talk to her."

"What happened?"

"Beats me. I guess she decided she'd enjoy having me out of the house for a while. Last week, I thought maybe she'd finally come back around when she started asking questions about you, but Dad — "

"Whoa. What do you mean she started asking questions about me?"

"Well, you know, about your diabetes and all. If he thought you were really up to the trip."

Randy pushed himself up on an elbow and tried to glare at me through the gloom. "Hey, look, man. I am up to any damn thing I want to be up to. Diabetes doesn't keep me down. I keep *it* down. Maybe I don't know the woods like you Eagle Scouts, but that's one thing you don't have to worry about."

"I didn't say that I was worried. She was. But Dad said it'd be okay, that you were an expert with all that diabetes stuff."

"Damned right I am."

He lay back, and neither of us said anything for a couple of minutes. "By the way," I said, "I wasn't an Eagle Scout. Bob was, but I only made it about half-way."

"Oh, that's reassuring. I thought you were Joe Nature. That's what my old man's been saying. 'Pay attention to Mark. Watch what he's doing. He knows the woods.' "

"I don't. Not much, anyway."

He groaned. "Thanks for telling me now. God, I wonder if it's too late to break a leg."

I almost laughed. "Hey, could you do that? I mean, I could hit you with the blunt edge of the ax or something."

"Shut up and go to sleep."

I thought for a moment. "So you really haven't been camping or anything before?"

"Last question, last answer. No, not unless you count sleeping in a tent in the backyard or going for a walk in the park. Otherwise, *nada*. Nothing. And I never wanted to."

"Then why didn't you just say you wouldn't go?"

"Look, I told you that was the last question for tonight. Let's just say it's because I'm a good little boy who does things because my pappy and grandpappy did them."

"Family tradition, huh?"

"Something like that. Now, for God's sake, let me get some sleep. If I'm going to slog through the wilderness with some Turkey Scout, or whatever you were, I need some Z's." He turned over.

"First Class," I said. "That's about halfway to Eagle."

"Whatever. Go to sleep."

I lay with my hands behind my head for a few minutes more, watching the glow of the firelight. So why the hell was I here? Mainly because I'd been too damned chicken to admit that I was a wimp — or too much wimp to admit that I was a chicken — before it was too late. And, now, we were in for it. I pulled the sleeping bag around my shoulders and curled up. Out in the night, a loon called, its cry cold and lonely across the dark waters stretching north.

12

CHAPTER TWO

Dad shook the tent pole. "Roll out and roll 'em up, boys! Daylight in the swamp."

"Okay, okay," I groaned. "We're up." He stopped shaking the tent, and I heard him walking across to where Uncle Jerry was rattling pans at the fire.

"What the hell was that all about?" Randy mumbled.

I sat up, shivering in the chill, and started pulling on my sweatshirt. "The lumberjack wake-up call. Dad read it in a book last year and hasn't forgotten it since."

"God, that must have gotten old quick." He sat up groggily, and I caught him square in the chest with an elbow. He said, "Ooff," and slumped back.

"Sorry," I said. "You okay?"

"I think so, but I won't make that mistake again. From here on in, one of us gets dressed at a time. But hurry up, I've gotta take a leak." He pointed at one of my boots. "Uh, you might want to empty that before you put it on. I needed to go in the night, but I didn't want my richard getting bit up by the mosquitoes."

"Very funny," I said, pulling on the boot.

"Hmmm. Must have been the other one."

13

"Maybe it was one of yours. Are you always this funny in the morning?"

"Just until I get my shot. Come on, get your big ass outta here; I'm about to explode."

I don't like jokes about the size of my butt or my belly, and I snapped at him, "Watch it, shrimp."

"Shrimp? Hell, I'm as tall as you are."

"Yeah, but you're still a runt."

I crawled out through the flap, adroitly kneeing the pole so that the tent collapsed on him. "Hey, damn it!" he yelped.

"Oops, sorry." I propped the pole back in position and, feeling better, walked over to the bushes to take a whiz.

"Pancakes are on, boys," Uncle Jerry called.

"I'm coming," Randy yelled. "Don't let hippo-boy eat 'em all before I get there." Dad and Uncle Jerry laughed, and I glared at the tent. Okay, Charlie, next time I'll roll you up in that damned tent and dump you in the lake. I zipped my fly and gazed balefully at my gut hanging over my belt. God, I really did have to lose twenty pounds. I was getting tired of sucking it in, particularly around Sonia. Okay, starting today. Might as well accomplish something on this damned trip.

Dad pointed to the penciled line stretching from our campsite to a point at the far northeastern corner of the lake. "Okay, you're here and the portage to Cedar Lake is there. What course are you going to paddle?"

I felt a jolt of panic. "Aren't you going with us? I thought you were going to tow us over there with the motorboat."

"Nope. We're going to catch lunch. You and Randy have a shakedown cruise, and we'll see you over there around noon. So, come on, what's your course to the portage?"

I clumsily positioned my compass on the chart and managed to get a bearing. "Uh, about zero-three-zero, I make it."

"Pretty close," he said. "Now you don't want to keep looking at your compass every five minutes, so try to find a landmark."

I stood, held the compass out in front of me as I'd been taught, and sighted along it to the distant shore. "Maybe that little island? I think the portage must be behind it."

"Behind it?"

"Uh, I think so."

"What's the map tell you?" I looked at the map. The island was a good quarter mile to the west of the portage. I felt myself redden. Dad sighed. "Look, it's okay. You'll get the hang of it." He grinned. "You might paddle a few extra miles, but you'll eventually get where you're going."

"Maybe," I said.

"Confidence, Mark. Okay, so you know you want to keep the island on your left. That's a good start. When you're halfway across the lake, take another sighting to get a landmark closer to the portage. Do that a time or two more, and pretty soon you'll spot the landing. We'll have fish frying when you get there." I nodded glumly.

"We're about ready here," Uncle Jerry called from the shore, where he and Randy were loading the canoe.

"Coming," Dad called. He slapped my back hard enough to make me stumble. "Come on, voyageur. Time to get on the water. No turning back now."

Randy took his seat gingerly in the bow, and I only slightly less shakily in the stern. The lake looked immense, an unimaginable reach of blue flecked with whitecaps between us and the distant green shore leveled almost to a line by distance and the weight of the haze-gray sky. For a moment, the colors had me, and I fumbled through my mental paint box, trying to imagine how I'd mix that gray, that green, that exact cold blue if I had tubes of oils and a feel for paint. But then Uncle Jerry gave a grunt and a shove, and we were floating free of the shore.

"Put the ash to 'er, boys," Dad called. "We'll see you at noon."

"Put the what to what?" Randy asked.

"Paddle to the water."

"Another quaint saying, huh?"

"You got it. Well, let's do it."

Despite the practice we'd had in the last two days, Randy still didn't have the paddling down, and I had trouble timing my strokes to his. "Don't cherry-pick," I called. "Remember what my dad said about not letting your right hand swing any higher than your eyes." He bobbed his head and started getting a better stroke with less motion. I got in rhythm with him, ending every third stroke with a twist of the wrist — what Dad called a J-stroke — to keep the canoe straight. Ahead I could see whitecaps rolling east toward the head of the lake and knew that the wind was waiting to give a couple of city boys a hard time once we hit open water.

I hadn't guessed the half of it. The wind grabbed the bow the instant we cleared the point of land to the west. I quit doing the J-stroke and dug hard to keep us straight. But that didn't do it, and in seconds, we'd yawed wildly off course. "Why are we turning?" Randy hollered. "I thought the portage was over there." He waved a hand toward the northeast.

"We're turning because I can't figure out how to keep the SOB straight! The wind's too strong." I threw my weight into another hard stroke that did no good.

He gestured toward the campsite. "Well, the old guys sure think it's pretty damned funny." I looked. I couldn't hear them, but Dad and Uncle Jerry were obviously enjoying the hell out of the spectacle. Uncle Jerry was bent over, holding his stomach, while Dad made wild gestures with his arms. "I think your dad's trying to show you a stroke," Randy said.

I squinted, trying to figure out the pinwheeling of Dad's arms. Something he'd called a sweep? Worth a try. I reached my paddle out as far as I could and pulled it through the water in an arc, my muscles popping with the strain. The bow edged back into the wind. "Okay," I yelled, "that'll work. Paddle on my side, but lean the other way a little or we'll dump this damned thing."

He did as I told him, and together we muscled the bow around until we were heading north again. I glanced over my shoulder at Dad and Uncle Jerry. They were standing, hands on hips, watching us go. And I knew they were still chuckling. Turkeys.

We pushed on toward the middle of the lake, the whitecaps slapping against the aluminum hull. Randy leaned into his strokes, occasionally flinging water back over the packs. "Hey," I snapped. "Don't do that, huh?"

"Do what?"

"Splash everything. Me included."

He turned to look. "Did I do that?"

"Damn straight."

"Sorry. Too much backswing, I guess."

"Just don't get in the habit."

He shrugged. "Aye, aye, captain."

For the next half hour, we paddled without talking. I could feel a knot stinging high in my left shoulder and sweat breaking through the back of my shirt. The sun's heat had yet to burn away the gray haze, and the wind made the sweat feel like a ribbon of ice down my spine. I imagined that wind coming to life over a snow-field somewhere high in the Rockies and then sweeping across a thousand miles of plains before blowing into the forest and lake country of northern Minnesota, where even on this late August day it still had enough of the chill of snow to gray the sunshine and to turn the water a cold blue-green.

"Hey, Mark!"

"Huh?" I looked at Randy, who'd turned halfway around in his seat and was staring at me. "What?"

"I asked if we could switch sides for a while. My shoulder's getting tired."

"Yeah, sure." We switched and started paddling again. Careful, I told myself. That's the second time this morning.

I have this problem concentrating sometimes. I can

18

be doing almost anything, mowing the lawn, sitting in class, or walking home from school, when suddenly my mind sort of strolls off on its own. It's usually a color or how light plays on something that gets me. Mom calls it woolgathering, Dad calls it spacing out. It irritates them some, especially because more than one teacher has mentioned it on my report card. But only Bob makes a real big deal out of it. Bob says I'm "drifty" — which is apparently a major crime in ROTC and something that Bob stomps every chance he gets as a cadet officer. I know; he practices the stomping on me every time he's home on vacation.

I'm better now that I've quit painting and dumped my oils and watercolors in a corner of the attic for the next time we have a garage sale. (And before you start thinking the world lost the next van Gogh or Picasso when I quit painting, I'll mention that I was no damned good at it, anyway. I've got Bob's opinion, my art teacher's, and my own to prove it.) But color and light still get me sometimes.

I squinted across the chop of the whitecaps, trying to spot the island I'd picked as a landmark. If we could get in the lee, we could take a rest. But despite our efforts to stay on course, the wind had pushed us too far to the east. Crap. "Just keep paddling," I called. "I've got to use the compass."

I pulled the compass from around my neck and tried to sight along it through the spray coming off Randy's paddle and the roll of the canoe. And between balancing my own weight and trying to remember everything Dad had told me about taking a sighting, I fumbled the son of a bitch. "Shit!" I screamed, clawing for the cord as the compass bounced off the gunwale and hit the water with a fatal little plop.

"Hey!" Randy yelped. "Cripes, you almost turned us over." I stared at the glimmer of silver fading out of sight far beneath the canoe. "What happened?" he asked.

"I dropped the damned compass. Dad is going to be pissed."

Randy peered over the side, more curious than sympathetic. "Cost a lot?"

"Twenty bucks or so."

"Hmmm. Well, better you did it now than later, I guess. We can't really get lost between here and the portage, can we?"

I gazed at the spot on the far shore where I thought the portage should be. "I guess not. . . ." I stared a final time into the depths, wondering if fish would pause to stare curiously at the dial of my compass, fluorescent in the blackness as it settled on the bottom fifty or a hundred feet down, its needle forever pointing north. Then I swung the bow back on course for the portage, the blade of my paddle leaving behind a swirl like a miniature whirlpool in the cold blue-green of the water.

I followed Dad to the beach. He held out his compass, and I took it, not meeting his eyes. He cleared his throat. "So, not the best of starts."

"I'm sorry, Dad. I didn't drop it on purpose."

He didn't reply for a moment, which told me that he'd at least considered the possibility. "No, of course not. But you shouldn't have taken it off your neck.

20

That's why I put a good long cord on it. You can't ever be without a compass and matches out here. They taught you that in Boy Scouts." I nodded. He slapped me on the shoulder. "Okay, forget about the compass. Just take it as a lesson." He glanced at the sun. "Well, you guys have got quite a ways to go today. Come on. We'll get you across the first portage."

I nodded, all my plans for a last-minute appeal to common sense gone with my compass. We were going to have to do this, like it or not. I followed him back to the fire, where Uncle Jerry and Randy were putting away the lunch dishes.

My knees almost buckled under the weight of the pack. "Got it?" Dad asked.

"Sort of. This is the heavy one, isn't it?"

"They're both about the same. Jerry and I'll take the canoe."

"Thanks." I lumbered toward the trail where Randy waited, the pack on his back looking suspiciously light.

We were both puffing hard by the time we stumbled to the top of a low ridge and got our first look at Cedar Lake. Behind us, Dad shouted, "Keep moving, boys. Remember, just like a couple of marines."

"Just like a couple of idiots," I panted.

Randy grunted. "You've got that right." He hitched up his pack and started down the slope. Well, at least we agreed on something, but that didn't keep me from hoping he'd trip and sprain an ankle. He didn't.

Dad and Uncle Jerry flipped the canoe off their shoulders and set it on the stony beach. They straightened their backs, grumping good-naturedly about not being as young as they used to be. "Now, boys," Dad said, "I want you to remember — "

Uncle Jerry broke in. "Give 'em a break, Ed. They've heard it all before."

Dad laughed. "I guess they have. Well, nothing left to do other than wish you *bon voyage.*" He came over to us and shook our hands. There was something in his eyes — something both joyful and fierce — that made me swallow. "Good luck, son," he said. "Have a great time."

"Uh, thanks, Dad. We'll do our best."

Uncle Jerry shook my hand and then gave Randy a quick hug. "Stay dry and don't tangle with the bears," he said.

"Don't worry," Randy said.

Dad had paused to mess with a pack strap. "For God's sake, stop fussing, Ed," Uncle Jerry called. "They're going to be fine, and we've got fish to catch." Dad laughed again, tugged a final time on the strap, and together they headed down the trail toward Cant Hook, the boat, and a lazy week at the resort.

Randy slapped a mosquito. "Well, now what, admiral?"

"I guess we could camp here for a few days and then sneak back to the resort."

"Not a bad idea, but I think they'd figure it out."

"Yeah, probably." I glanced at my watch and then unfolded the map. "Well, we're supposed to paddle across this lake and then do a short portage to the next lake north. . . . Uh, here it is. Little Crim Lake. We're supposed to camp there."

Randy followed my finger on the map, and then gazed skeptically across the lake. "You mean the portage is way the hell over there at the other end of the lake? We're going to be heading straight into the wind all the way."

"You got it. How'd you feel about getting real sick right now? I could chase after them, and we could get out of this yet."

He glared at me, real anger in his eyes. "Don't expect me to wimp out, jerk. I never use the Big D as an excuse. Not ever. Got it?" He stomped away, shoved the canoe into the water, and reached for one of the packs.

"Sorry," I said. "Just kidding."

"Just help me load the canoe, huh?"

I angled the bow to the right so that we didn't pitch with every whitecap, but we were still making one stroke of progress for every three. Gulls and ducks bobbed off to our left, too smart to try flying in the stiff wind from the west. "This is nuts," I yelled. "I'm going to steer for that island. We'll take a rest behind it and then try to sneak along the north shore. It might be better over there."

"I need a granola bar first." He turned in his seat and dug into the side pocket of the pack behind him. "Damn. Wrong pack. Reach into that one and grab me one of those cherry ones, huh?"

I was fighting to hold the bow on our new course. "Wait until we get behind the island. Then you can have all the snacks you want."

He gave me an annoyed look. "No, you don't understand, man. When I say I need a bar, I mean I *need* one. Otherwise, my blood sugar level goes to hell, and you can forget about me doing anything up here except maybe fainting and falling over the side." I must have looked shocked or scared at that, because he grimaced. "Relax. It doesn't happen quite that fast, but I do need a bar, man."

"Coming right up," I said. "Try to hold the bow for a minute." I dug into the side pocket of the pack, found a granola bar, and tossed it to him.

He took his time eating it, while I fought to keep us from losing any more progress. Finally, he crumpled the wrapper and picked up his paddle. "Okay, let's go."

We rested in the lee of the island. I broke down and had a Snickers. Hell of a start to the diet, but I figured the paddling had already vaporized about a week's calories. Randy experimented with sitting on one of the boat cushions but didn't like the added height and shoved it back under the seat.

"Seems like they could have given us something a little classier for life preservers," he said. "What good are these going to be?"

I shrugged. "They meet the law and they're handy to sit on in camp."

"Speaking of which, are we really going to make it to that next lake today?"

I glanced at the sun. "Not unless we get going. Ready?"

"I guess."

Hugging the north shore, we managed to get out of the worst of the wind. And, given different company, I might have enjoyed the sunshine and the scenery. I

24

tried to imagine Sonia sitting in Randy's place in the bow. Yeah, that'd be nice. Real nice.

I shivered just remembering how she'd looked in that two-piece suit, her blond hair falling wet over her brown shoulders, when she'd come out of the wave pool at Cosmic Wave — America's biggest indoor-outdoor water park. (*Come see our amaaazing sliiiding roof. Get your tan under summer sun. Stay warm and wet when summer's done.*)

Now Cosmic Wave is about the last place in Minneapolis — or the world for that matter — that I'd go for entertainment. But Mom wanted some time to try on clothes without Quentin and Beth terrorizing the mall. So she laid some heavy persuasion on me in the form of money, and I like money slightly more than I hate water. All of which explains how come I was sitting on the concrete beach, watching my ten-year-old brother and sister splashing in the wave pool, when I caught sight of Sonia coming out of the water in that two-piece suit. A couple of boys, maybe eight and nine, were trailing her and whining. Sonia snapped, "Go ahead. Stay in the water. Just stop beating on each other. I've had enough." She stretched out on a towel a dozen feet from me and stared moodily at the waves.

"Baby-sitting?" I asked.

She turned her head to squint at me. "Oh, hi. Yeah, stupid little monsters. Mom gets to go shopping, I get the kids."

"Same deal for me. The twin brats over there are my brother and sister. Want to trade?"

She gazed at them. "Nah, they look even worse." She squinted at me again. "Say, I know you, don't I?"

"Sort of. I'm Mark Severson. We were in biology together."

She dug around in her beach bag for her glasses and put them on. "Oh, yeah. I remember you now. You sat a couple of tables over from me."

"Right. With . . ." I started to reel off the names, caught myself — no sense in mentioning any geeky friends — and said, "a couple of other guys."

"Did you like that class?"

"Not particularly." Hell, I didn't like any of my classes. Hadn't in years.

"God, I hated it. I told my mom that I'd quit school if she ever made me take another class where I had to touch something slimy."

"I know what you mean," I said, wishing that I could think of something witty to say on the subject of dissecting worms and crayfish.

Sonia stared balefully at her brothers. "And speaking of slimy, I hate this." She sat up, and I got a shot of cleavage that curled my toenails. "To heck with it," she said. "The lifeguards will save 'em if they start to drown. I'm going down a couple of slides. Want to come?"

"Sure," I said, hardly believing that I'd agree to anything that stupid.

We climbed to the top of the Blue Python, this insane thing where the coils alternately narrow and widen as you shoot down about four hundred yards of tunnel before going airborne for a drop of about fifty feet into a pool. Not my idea of fun, and I'd just about lost my nerve by the time we reached the top of the ladder. Sonia gave me a big grin. "Want to go together?"

"Uh, sure." I got awkwardly onto the slide and put my arms tentatively around her waist as the lifeguard gestured that we could go.

"Hold on tight," Sonia yelled. And, boy, did I, as we went screaming down the Python to be shot into thin air for the plunge into the pool, where I would have drowned happy if she hadn't slipped out of my arms.

I climbed out of the pool after her. "Wheee-ooh!" she yelled. "That was great!" She grabbed my arm. "Which one shall we do next?"

Could we just go someplace and get naked? I thought. "I don't care," I said. "You choose."

We did another half dozen slides before it was time to get the kids out of the wave pool and across the street to the mall and their mommies. On the way to the locker rooms, I asked, "Do you want to get a Coke or something after we get rid of the kids?"

"Sure. Why not?"

I know that wasn't the most enthusiastic answer any guy ever got from a girl, but it set me walking on air. Maybe Sonia had only a vague memory of me from biology class, but I'd memorized every detail about her. I didn't exactly have a crush on her — not any more than I had a crush on about half the girls in the freshman class — but she definitely revved my hormones. I'd never called her, of course, figuring that she was way out of my league. But maybe her eyesight was just bad enough that she wouldn't spot a walking social disaster. Or at least not right away. Suck in your gut, I told myself, and lay on whatever charm you've got. This is the chance of the summer.

Fortunately, she did most of the talking over the table at Mac's, and I didn't have much to do except smile, agree, and sympathize. Apparently that was enough, because when I finally got up the courage to ask if she'd like to catch a movie, she said, "Sure. Why not?"

We started hanging around pretty steady over the next couple of weeks. We cruised the mall, saw a couple of movies, got in on a couple of parties, and made out a couple of times — not real heavy but enough to give me hope. And, for the first time in a very long time, I was feeling just a little bit good about myself.

You see, gorgeous girls were always hanging on Bob, but I'd never had a bit of luck before. Hell, even the plain ones told me after a date or two that they weren't desperate enough to go out with me again. (Maybe not in so many words, but close.) I'd gotten so frustrated that I'd even made the very big mistake of complaining about it to Mom. She patted me on the shoulder. "Don't worry, dear. Your brother started too young, and I always worried. The right girl will come along for you someday. Be patient." Thanks a lot, Ma. *Just* what I wanted to hear.

So even if Sonia wasn't exactly one of Bob's cheerleader types, she made me happy. Real happy — until I had to tell her about this stupid trip. I expected her to be a little sad or maybe even a little put out, but instead she acted like she didn't give a damn. *Oh, okay. Well, we'll see you around, sweetie.* Sort of like that.

So here I was a week later in this godforsaken country with Randy and about ten billion bugs, while Sonia worked on her tan in Minneapolis between runs down the Blue Python. And I sure wasn't the only guy with eyes to notice how she filled out the top of that bathing suit. Damn.

The sun was falling toward the trees by the time we beached the canoe at the portage. Randy climbed out and wandered up onto the shore. "Hey, Randy. Hold the bow, huh?" I called.

"Oh, yeah. Sure."

He came back and held it while I struggled over the packs until I could step out onto dry land. While I worked the kinks out of my legs and shoulders, he sat on a log and started messing with his blood tester. He glanced at me. "You know, there are some other things you could do besides standing around watching me. Like finding a campsite. I, for one, sure don't feel like doing another portage today."

I felt like saying, "Hey, I haven't watched you yet, man. That needle stuff gives me the creeps." But I decided not to admit it. "Sure," I said.

The beach was too narrow and rocky for a tent, so I made my way up the trail. The land on either side fell away into brushy swamp, but a couple of hundred feet from the beach I found a spot where somebody had wedged a tent off the trail on some slightly higher ground.

Back at the canoe, Randy was still messing around with his tester. "I found a place," I said. "It's not the greatest, but we're only staying overnight. We can cook down here."

"Sounds good to me. Who builds the fire and who sets up the tent?"

29

I shrugged. "Your choice."

He clutched his chest. "I get choices on this trip?"

"Yeah, why not?" God, he got weird sometimes.

"Just surprised to know it. Okay, I'll get the fire going."

He went to gather some sticks while I lugged the tent pack up the trail. I had the tent half up when the wind decided to call it a day. Two seconds later, I was engulfed in a cloud of mosquitoes. I grabbed the bug dope and fled.

Randy was alternately slapping at mosquitoes and trying to light a pile of sticks. He looked up. "You got the repellent? The bugs are coming out."

I shook a few drops of dope onto my palms and tossed the bottle to him. "They're a hell of a lot worse back in the woods. They weren't stupid enough to try flying in the wind, they just rested up, waiting for us."

"Well, maybe the smoke will drive them away." He rearranged his pile of sticks and lit another match.

I hesitated. "Well, I guess I'll go finish. Unless you'd rather."

"Dream on. I've got a fire to build."

When I got back, considerably bumpier, he was sitting on his haunches, swearing under his breath. About two dozen burned matches lay around the pile of cold sticks. "Okay, Joe Nature, what'd I do wrong? I thought I had it going and then it fizzled."

I knelt beside him. "I think you're rushing it. You've got to start with twigs, not these big sticks. Some bark would help, too." I sorted through his pile of branches and found enough smaller stuff.

Maybe I hadn't learned a lot in Boy Scouts, but I

managed to get a decent fire going after a couple of tries. Randy didn't comment on my skill, only grunted sourly and began getting out stuff for supper. He studied the menu Uncle Jerry had written for us. "Spaghetti tonight, I guess. Sound okay?"

"Yeah, that's fine." I added a couple of larger sticks to the fire.

If anyone ever invites you over for a meal of freeze-dried spaghetti, take a miss. The stuff is terrible. We boiled the water for five minutes, remembering what Uncle Jerry had said about the beaver and duck crap in lake water giving you the runs for about two weeks. Then we cut off the top of the spaghetti pouch, poured in the right amount of water — more or less — and waited the required five minutes. The resulting glop looked, smelled, and tasted like dog food with tomato sauce. After a few bites, Randy looked at me. "This stuff is really bad. You any good at catching fish?"

"Went a few times with Dad, but never caught much. You?"

"Never even tried. But I'm gonna start learning tomorrow."

I set down my plate. "Then I guess I'll go hungry until you land the big one."

He looked into his plate again. "Well, I wish I had a choice, but I don't." He stuck a forkful of spaghetti in his mouth and chewed. After a minute, I picked up my plate. If he could, I could.

It was nearly dark when we remembered to hang the food pack. We had a hell of a time doing it, mostly because neither of us had paid close attention to Uncle

Jerry's instructions. Finally, we managed to get it slung between two trees. Randy reached up on tiptoes. "I can still touch it. Do you think a bear can?"

"I don't know. Maybe a big one."

"I think my dad would tell us to get it higher."

"It's not going any higher with this rig. Do you want to start over?"

He gazed at the swinging pack uncertainly. "Nah, it'll probably be all right."

We sat by the fire, drinking cocoa before braving the scurry through the bugs to the tent. The boiled lake water gave the cocoa a smoky taste that wasn't entirely unpleasant after a couple of swallows. I pulled on the old leather glove we had for a pot holder. "There's a little left. Want some?"

"Nah, go ahead," Randy said. "I've got plenty." He leaned back against a log and stared at the stars.

I emptied the pot into my cup and settled back. Out on the lake, a loon popped to the surface at the edge of the campfire's reflection. It stared at us, the red of its eyes flashing in the firelight, then gave its strange, unearthly cry. Randy jumped a foot, spilling cocoa on his knee. He swore some.

"Just a loon," I said. "You can just see him."

"I know it's a loon," he snapped. "I just wish to God they didn't sneak around doing that when you're not expecting it."

The loon cried again and then dove. "Yeah, they do sound kind of spooky." I slapped another mosquito. "Let's get in the tent. The bugs are getting worse."

Randy blew on his scalded knee. "Suits me."

We spent fifteen minutes killing the mosquitoes in

the tent and then turned off the flashlight. Randy burrowed into his sleeping bag. "Damn, it gets cold up here at night."

"Yeah, it does."

"God, if I ever warm up, I'm really going to sleep. I'm beat."

I lay on my back, thinking. "Randy, you got a girl?"

"Cripes," he said. "Don't start talking about girls now. I don't want to be cold *and* horny."

"Yeah, but do you have a girl?"

"Nobody steady, put it that way. And, since you're bound to tell me anyway, I might as well ask if you do."

"Sort of," I said. "Her name's Sonia. We've been going out for a few weeks."

"And you're worried she's not going to be waiting when you get back."

I bristled. "I didn't say that."

He grunted. "Well, that's what you're thinking."

"How do you know?"

"Because I can read your mind. Now go to sleep." He shifted around, trying to get comfortable, then paused. "And, hey, if you happen to start dreaming, don't forget it's me not your girl over on this side of the tent. I tend to react violently when somebody gets too friendly when I'm sleeping."

"Oh? You've had a problem with that before? Who's been feeling you up at night?"

"Your girl. Now go to sleep."

"Hey, you're the one doing most of — "

"Mark," he said, "shut up."

Well, I didn't want to talk to him anyway, so I did as I was told.

CHAPTER
THREE

Gray fog lay on the lake, clammy tatters drifting over the shore to mix with the smoke of our cooking fire. We dawdled over breakfast, listening to the clouds of insects already humming in the swamp on either side of the narrow trail to Little Crim Lake.

Randy finished his orange juice and started gathering the plates together. "I don't feel much like a marine," he said, "but I guess we're going to have to do it sometime."

"I guess. Shall we take the boat or come back for it?"

Randy imitated Dad. "That's a canoe, Mark. Not a boat."

"But it floats, Daddy," I whined. "Doesn't that make it a boat?"

"It's a canoe, you stupid little shit. How many times I gotta tell you that?"

I laughed. "You do him pretty well."

"Yeah, I had to listen to you bitching at each other for two days."

"Were we that bad?"

34

"Nah, not really. Just about the map and the compass. Don't worry about it."

I gazed up the trail. "Well, I guess we could try it with the canoe. Beats hanging the food pack an extra time."

Randy shrugged. "You're the boss."

"Stop saying that," I said, and went to start packing up the tent and sleeping bags.

We weren't very efficient yet, and it was after nine before we were ready to go. We helped each other on with the packs, managed to get the canoe on our backs, and lumbered up the trail. We had to move carefully on the thin grease of mud left by the rain of a couple of days before. The mosquitoes and blackflies sensed us and came swarming out of the swamp, boring in on our ears, eyes, and bare hands. Randy shook his head and tried to blow them away from his face. "Damn," he growled. "Let's put down the canoe and — "

Just then, I slipped, the weight of the pack throwing me to the left. I tried to get my balance, but by then Randy was losing his. We both had the same idea at the same instant and threw the canoe to the right as we ducked out to the left. Not graceful. Randy caught hold of a tree while I landed on my butt in the mud, and the canoe hit with a metallic boom that Dad and Uncle Jerry probably heard on Cant Hook.

"What happened?" Randy asked.

"I slipped. Sorry. You okay?"

"Yeah. How about you?"

"I'm okay. Feel kind of like a turtle on his back, but all the parts are still working." I tried to stand, but the weight of the pack toppled me backward onto my butt.

Randy held out his hands. "Grab hold." I did, and he leaned back while I got my feet under me. Then his feet slipped, and we were both sitting in the mud. "Oh, hell," he said. He leaned back against his pack and slapped at a mosquito, his hand leaving a muddy smudge on his cheek. "This isn't working out."

"Yeah, I noticed."

He stared up at the patch of gray sky visible through the overhanging trees. "You know, I'd almost think this was funny if we didn't have another week to go."

I sighed. "Maybe we should just give up now before we really get in trouble."

"Is that what you really want to do?"

"Do you?"

"I asked you first."

I shrugged. "Yeah, that's what I'd like to do, but I don't think I'd better. Dad wouldn't give me any slack for months. Hell, he wouldn't let me out of the house after dark."

Randy waved at the cloud of bugs around his head. "Yeah, same with me. Worse, maybe. And I'd have to put up with Marcia knowing that I'm a bigger wimp than she already thinks I am."

"Marcia thinks you're a wimp?"

He shrugged. "She's twelve and thinks all boys are wimps."

"I wish that was the worst my brother thought of me. Every month or so he writes me a letter telling me how I've got to get my shit together and stop making things so tough on Mom and Dad. Which really pisses me off, because I don't think I'm that hard to live with,

36

I've just got my own ways of doing things. But he figures he knows just exactly how to run my life."

"Yeah, that sounds like Bob the — "

I slapped at a mosquito diving for my ear and missed the last word. "What? I didn't get that."

"I just said that sounds like Bob. Or at least how I remember him."

"Yeah, but what'd you call him?"

"Forget it. Just a nickname I had for him."

"Hey, there isn't anything you can call my brother that'd piss me off other than maybe your hero."

He shrugged. "I used to call him Bob the Nazi."

I stared at him and then started laughing so hard tears came to my eyes.

Randy smiled. "Fits, huh?"

"Oh, God, you don't know the half of it. I should have thought of it." I started laughing again, and Randy joined me.

Finally, he got his breath. "You know, boss, this is a really weird place to have a conversation. The bugs may be enjoying it, but my ass is wet and I'm feeling a significant loss of blood. If we don't get out of here pretty quick, they're going to carry us off into the swamp, cocoon us, and feed on our bodies all winter." He got an arm around a tree, struggled to his feet, and reached out a hand to help me up.

I shook my head. "That didn't work worth a damn last time." I slid my butt across the mud until I could grab hold of a tree and managed to stand. "Cocoon us? You've got a really weird sense of humor."

"At least I've got one. That's saying something for anyone related to you and Bob."

"Me? Come on, I've got a great sense of humor."

"Uh-huh. So, are we going forward or going back?"

I hesitated a final time. "Forward, I guess. This trip wasn't my idea, but it looks like we've got to prove we can do it."

He nodded. "Yeah, it looks like."

"Let's get the packs across and come back for the canoe. The mud's too slippery to try both at once."

"Suits me. Lead on, *el capitán*."

Little Crim was shallow and green, hardly more than a flooded swamp surrounded by thick brush. Randy shrugged out of his pack and let it thud to the ground. His shirt was soaked with sweat, and it took him a moment to get his breath. "Are we really going to hang the food pack?" he asked.

I hesitated, studying the brush along the shore. "Hell, we'll only be gone a few minutes. Let's just chance it."

We hustled back, grabbed the canoe, and did our best to jog — very carefully — back to the packs. "You paranoid?" I panted.

"Yeah. We shouldn't have done that."

The food pack was standing untouched where we'd left it. We swung the canoe off our shoulders. Randy started coughing hard, and I had a lurch of fear. "You okay?"

"Yeah, yeah. Just swallowed a bug." He hacked and spat.

"Let's get out of here. I think the bugs have called for reinforcements."

"I'm with you."

We were nearly in the middle of the lake before the bugs let up enough for us to take a break. Randy shipped his paddle and swung his feet over the seat so he sat facing me. "You know," he said, "maybe we should go by the rules on that food pack. I had this image of a whole family of bears splitting up the grub. You've got something to live on, but that'd be a bad deal for me."

We'd been friendly all morning, and his comment caught me by surprise. "Hey, I've got a sense of humor for a lot, but I don't appreciate comments about my gut."

He looked at me in surprise. "I didn't mean it that way. I've got to have food or I'm in big trouble. Don't be so damned sensitive."

I was about to tell him where he could stick "sensitive" when the water suddenly roiled just to the right of the bow. I had a brief glimpse of a brown body before it disappeared with a slap like a gunshot. Randy nearly jumped out of his boots, and I had to steady the canoe. "What the hell was that?" he yelped.

"Beaver, I think." I searched the surface of the lake, picking out the beaver as he broke the surface forty or fifty feet from the canoe. "Look, over there. He's going to do it again." The beaver went under with a slap of its broad tail.

"Is he pissed or something? Trying to scare us away?"

"Could be, I guess." I searched the marshy shoreline. "See that mound of sticks? I'll bet you that's his home."

"Looks like the pictures in the books, all right."

"Want to go have a look?"

"Suppose he attacks?"

39

"I don't think they attack. They get their revenge by crapping in the water and making canoers sick."

Randy looked uncertain. "If you say so. . . . Well, okay, Joe Nature, let's go have a look."

It wasn't very exciting, just a mound of mud and sticks, their ends chewed like pencils sharpened with a jackknife. The beaver cruised back and forth on the lake behind us, slapping its tail now and then. "I don't think he's happy," Randy said.

"I'm not an expert on beaver emotions, but I think you're right. Well, I guess we've seen all there is to see."

"Aren't you going to dive down to find the entrance?"

"Not in this lifetime. And definitely not in this water."

"Yeah, they must shit green."

"That's algae in the water," I said.

"Well, you believe what you want to believe, I'll believe what I want to believe. Which way now, admiral?"

I pointed toward the shore a few hundred yards to the northwest. "The trail is just over there."

"Joy, oh, joy," Randy said.

At the portage to Big Crim, we hung the food pack, carried the canoe across, and returned for the packs, the bugs chewing on us all the way.

We were halfway across Big Crim when the sun finally burned through the gray. I checked my watch. "Let's eat. We'll be back in the bugs as soon as we get near shore again."

"Okay," Randy said. He shipped his paddle, opened

the food pack, and dug out a couple of the high-energy lunches Uncle Jerry had bought for us at the outfitter's in Ely. He tossed one to me, and I slit it open with my jackknife.

There were three thick crackers that looked like they could break teeth, a cup of peanut butter and jelly, a bag of nuts and dried fruit, and a granola bar. "Wow," I said. "We are in fat city now."

"Maybe you are," Randy said.

I looked at him sharply, expecting to see his I-gotcha-again smirk, but he was struggling to get his lunch open. "Don't you have a knife?" I asked.

"Yeah, I've got a knife. Brand new one my old man gave me for my birthday. Trouble is, the SOB's with my spare blood meter in the trunk of the car. I hope he doesn't find it. That'd piss him off."

"Here." I held out my knife. "Don't miss or it'll go the way of my compass." I tossed it, and he caught it smoothly.

"Thanks." He unfolded the blade and slit the wrapping. "What's the entrée?"

"Come again?"

"Main course. Ah, here we are. Hardtack and peanut butter. Yum, yum."

"The biscuits look bad, but they're pretty good, actually."

He glanced at his watch. "Damn, I really ought to fire up the ol' Glucotron and check my blood before I eat this. . . . Oh, to hell with it. I'll check before my next snack."

When I'd finished the entrée — or whatever the hell

41

he'd called it — I leaned back and took my time with the fruit and nuts. "Hey, you've got to tell me why you started calling Bob 'the Nazi.' "

"If you want to know the truth, I didn't. It was *the Mom* who came up with it. Just used it once, but I never forgot it."

"When was this?"

"Way back. Remember those couple of summers when Grandpa was still alive and we had reunions at that resort near Winona?"

"Maple Grove Farm. Those were pretty good times."

"Yeah, they were. And do you remember that old barn they'd made into a rec center with shuffleboard, Ping-Pong, and pool?"

"Oh, sure. That barn was the best part of the whole place."

"Then you'll remember we weren't allowed to use the cues because we were too little but that we had fun just shoving the balls around and making up our own games."

"Sure. That was fun."

"Uh-huh. Except when Bob wanted to play."

I frowned. "I guess I don't remember that part."

"Well, I remember it real well, and it still pisses me off. Bob had a buddy, one of the other kids at the resort. Same kid both summers. And they'd just push in and take over. No by-your-leave, just 'beat it, you two, we're the hotshot pool players around here.' Remember now?"

I shrugged. "Vaguely. But Bob's always been like that."

42

"Uh-huh. Well, I went crying to *the Mom* about it one time. And she grumbled that Bob was a 'Nazi in training' and that he'd have better manners if he were her kid."

"And?"

"And I guess she told me to go find something else to do. Anyway, I liked the sound of 'Bob the Nazi,' even if I didn't know what a Nazi was. So I used it in front of Dad the first chance I got. And he just went apeshit. Told me never to call Bob that again and really read out *the Mom* about it that night. So I just used the nickname to myself from then on. Always remembered it, though."

"So your dad's a fan of Bob's, huh?"

"Oh, not that much. Not at all, come to think of it."

"Why do you say that?"

Randy shrugged. "Just some things he's said."

"Like what?"

"Just things." He looked out across the lake. "Maybe we ought — "

"Come on, Randy. What'd he say about Bob?"

Randy sighed. "Hey, I'm not sure you really want to hear all this. But we were talking on the drive up from St. Louis, and he said that he thought you got kind of the short end of the stick around your house. That you were caught in the middle, 'carrying Bob's equipment bag in one hand and the twins' diaper bag in the other.' That's how he put it, anyway."

"He's not far off."

"Well, he said that he figured this trip was a chance

for you to prove that you could do the same things Bob could. And that afterward maybe you'd feel better about yourself."

"Who says I feel bad about myself?" Other than me, I thought.

He shrugged. "I'm just repeating. I didn't say anything except that as far as I was concerned this middle-child thing is a lot of horseshit. It's toughest being first, like Bob and me, because we've got to teach parents everything. Middle kids are just a bunch of crybabies as far as we're concerned."

I stared at him openmouthed. "Now wait a goddamned second — "

He laughed. "Come on. I'm just putting you on." I grumped some and he said, "Hey, look. About the last thing my dad said was that one of these days Bob's going to drop his richard in the dirt and trip over it. And that'd be the best thing that ever happened to him because it'd teach him some humility. And that you'll have a right to laugh and he's gonna join in."

"He really said that?"

"Yep. And, by the way, I'm gonna think it's pretty damned funny, too." He crumpled up the wrappings from his lunch. "So what's the drill, boss?"

"Well, I guess we go face the bugs and another portage. We've got two more to do today if we're going to stay on schedule."

"Maybe we ought to do one more and call it quits. What difference does it make if we spend one less night on the big lake? I could give a major damn."

"Okay," I said, "one more and we'll hang it up for today."

*   *   *

An absolute cloud of blackflies met us at the foot of the trail to Halloran Lake. We backed the canoe quickly into the lake and stared at the narrow, muddy trail disappearing into the brush. "God, this is worse than the last one," Randy said. "Are you sure we're in the right place?"

I studied the map. "This is it. Right by that little river."

"Why don't we try paddling up it?"

I studied the map again and then looked uncertainly at the river. "It doesn't say we can't, but — "

"Well, it looks okay to me. If it doesn't work, it doesn't work. We can always turn around."

"I guess."

We renewed our coating of bug dope and headed up the river. The current was a hell of a lot stronger than it had looked from the lake, and around the second bend we had to start working through rocks and shallows. "We've got to go back," I yelled.

"Screw that! The lake's got to be around that next bend. Come on, paddle."

Midway through the bend, we ran hard aground. We were both panting like dogs on a hot day. "Oh, hell," I said. "Now what?" Randy sat with his shoulders slumped for a long minute. Then he rolled up his pants and put a foot wearily over the side. "Hey," I said. "Maybe we should take off our boots."

"Not me," he said. "I'd rather have wet boots than get skinned up."

I hesitated, then rolled up my pants, and stepped out. The water was freezing. "Cripes! It feels like the snow just melted!" Randy didn't reply, just started pulling the canoe upstream.

The river corkscrewed through a half dozen more turns. Every time the water got up to our knees and we started thinking about getting back in the canoe, we'd hit another stretch of shallows. So we went on slipping and staggering through swarms of bugs until we at last rounded a final bend and came out on Halloran Lake.

We dragged the canoe onto the bank. I felt like giving Randy a pretty good shot about bad ideas, but he was leaning over, both hands braced on the canoe, and looking like he was going to be sick. After about a minute, he reached slowly into the side pocket of the food pack and got out a granola bar. "Uh, I thought you said you were going to use that testing gizmo before you ate again," I said.

"It's called a Glucotron, you dumb shit. *Glu-co-tron.*" He stumbled onto the shore, sat, and — slow motion — began unwrapping the bar. I watched him, trying to remember everything Dad had told me about diabetes. It wasn't much. I pulled the canoe up another couple of feet and stood waiting for him while the mosquitoes and blackflies practiced kamikaze dives on my neck and ears. Randy finished the bar and put his head between his knees. He didn't move or pay any attention to the insects circling around him. I hesitated, stepped closer, and tried to fan them away with my hat.

For ten minutes, neither of us said anything. I studied the swampy shoreline, but couldn't see a single dry spot where we could set up a tent. I glanced at the sun. "Randy," I said carefully, "I know we kind of agreed that this would be it for the day, but I can't see any place to camp. The next portage is real short, and Ax Handle is supposed to be a lot nicer lake. You just ride, and I'll get us across the lake."

He roused himself from what seemed like a long way away. "Give me another minute or two, and I'll be all right."

"Go ahead and get in. You can relax while I paddle."

"Don't nursemaid me, man," he snapped. "I can handle anything you can."

And he did. After the first few strokes, his energy seemed to come back and he started doing his share. When we neared the north shore, I told him to let up so that I could study the map again. "I think there's a chance we can skip this next portage," I said. "The map's got a channel marked just to the east. Maybe there's been enough rain for us to get through."

"We tried that once. It didn't work worth a damn."

"This might be different. It's a channel, not a river. Let's give it a try."

"You're the boss, I'm just the peon."

I looked up from the map. "Look, you've been on this boss-admiral-*el capitán* crap all day. If you want to paddle stern and read the map, be my guest."

"Yeah, and I suppose you'd really let me do that."

"Why not?"

"Shit," he muttered, and turned away.

"Hey, why not, man?"

"Because the old guys made you the boss. That's what my dad told me, remember? 'Listen to Mark. Watch what Mark does. Mark knows the woods.' "

47

"Well, he might have said it, but that doesn't make it true. I don't know horseshit about the woods, and you're not laying all the decisions off on me. We make them together or we just sit."

"Oh, no, you don't. I learned my lesson back on that river. You're the Boy Scout and the big boss man. And, if we get through that channel without getting our feet wet, I'll call you captain, big chief, *sabib*, anything you want for the rest of the trip."

I folded the map. "Look, dope, let me make this just as clear as I can. We're in this together. I never asked to be leader, and I don't want to be. If you want to take the blame for going up the river, feel free. But I'm not going to start making all the decisions so that you can have a good time bitching at me when they don't work out."

He stared at me. "You're not kidding, are you?"

"No."

"We're co-captains?"

"That's the deal."

He shook his head. "Wow. I thought all along that you were going to try to push me around. Play Joe Nature, the big woodsman."

"Nope," I said. "All I want to do is get through this trip with the minimum hassle from you, the bears, and whatever else we run into. So, do we try that channel, or do we just sit here arguing until the bugs finish us off?"

"Okay, let's see if we can get through. Why not?"

The channel wound narrow and weedy between high banks of rushes, humming with mosquitoes. It branched, then branched again, and we were in a blind alley with no way out except back the way we'd come. We backwatered all the way to the last junction, took the other branch until it split again, guessed wrong, and within a hundred yards, ran aground. Again we backwatered out. I was no longer sure which way we'd come, and without anything definite to take a bearing on, the compass wasn't much use.

"It looks wider up here to the left," Randy called.

"Okay," I said, hoping for a little luck. I angled the bow, while Randy used his paddle like a pole to push us around the tight corner. There was a sudden furious squawking, and Randy screamed, "Back up, back up!"

I backwatered like crazy, forgetting that I didn't have a lot of clearance to the rear. The stern shot into the rushes behind me, sticking fast in gooey mud. Randy flailed at something with his paddle as the squawking rose to a crescendo. I spun in my seat, jammed my paddle into the mud, and pushed with all my weight. The stern came free with a jerk, and I lost my grip on the paddle, leaving it upright in the mud, two feet out of my reach. Randy slapped his paddle on the water. "Get away from me, damn it! I don't want your stupid eggs."

"Give me your paddle!" I yelled.

"Are you crazy? It's all that's keeping me alive!"

"Then do a reverse sweep on your right!"

"A what?"

"Shit. Just give me your damned paddle."

"No!"

Just then my paddle decided to keel toward me in the ooze. I reached out as far as I could and grabbed it, pushed off against the mud, and backwatered furiously until we'd slid twenty yards down the channel.

I caught my breath. "What the hell *were* they?" I asked.

"Ducks. *Killer* ducks."

"Ducks?"

"Yeah. Like those ducks they've got in parks. But bigger and meaner."

I stared at him. "Let me get this straight. We've been chased by ducks?"

"Yeah. Ducks. Like I said."

"Chased, panicked, and humiliated by ducks?"

He looked at me. "Uh, yeah, like I — "

I started laughing.

"Hey, easy for you to laugh. You weren't up here fighting them off."

"No. No, I wasn't. I didn't have to face death at the hands — no, God, the webbed feet — of *killer* ducks."

When I had to stop laughing or die of asphyxiation, Randy was glaring at me. "Beaks and wings," he said. "They weren't using their feet." That set me off again. He turned away huffily and started paddling.

It seemed that we'd finally found the main channel because the water got deeper and wider as we turned the next corner. I checked the compass. Yeah, we were headed in more or less the right direction. "Okay, hold 'er steady for a second," I called. "I think the rushes are thinning a little and I'm gonna try to get a peek over 'em."

I stood on tiptoes, and the sight that greeted me was like a whole other world. The broad waters of Ax

Handle Lake stretched bright, open, and bug free beyond the waving wall of green.

"See anything?" Randy asked.

"Yeah, the big lake." I sat. "Go ahead, take a look."

He stood, a little uncertain of his balance. "Hey, that looks a lot better."

"That's what I thought."

"Think it's a mirage?"

"Might be. Or it might be for real. Let's find out."

The vision of the big lake kept us going as we plowed into another blind alley, backtracked, and finally broke through the rushes into open water. A breeze smelling of pine blew away the bugs and the stench of swamp. The shoreline rose, studded with granite outcroppings and tall pines, while the water went clear blue all the way down to a sandy bottom. Even the sun seemed warmer in a broad sky dotted with powder-puff clouds. "Hey," I said, "it's real."

"Yeah, like a different zone altogether, man. I thought it was getting on toward suppertime but here it's midafternoon. What time is it, anyway? I think my watch got drowned back in the river."

I glanced at my watch. "Three-thirty. I thought it was later, too."

"That means we don't have to hurry. Can you hold it for a second? I've got to check my blood."

"Sure," I said. He swung his legs around and sat facing me as he started to fiddle with his tester. "Glu-co-tron," I pronounced carefully.

He glanced up, puzzled for a second. Then he grinned. "Oh, yeah. I'd kind of forgotten about that.

Sorry. I just get a little edgy sometimes. It's a blood sugar thing. I was down then, now I may be a little high. So I've got to check." He got out the needle gizmo. "Ducks from Hell," he said.

"Huh?"

"That's what we'll name the movie: *Ducks from Hell*. Two guys up here in the Boundary Waters hunted by satanic ducks. Low budget, lots of gore."

"Better make it a canoeing party of eight or ten. Some people have got to get eaten."

"True. We can write that in."

"And babes," I said. "Gotta have at least one nude bathing scene before the ducks start to get them."

"Hey, there's hope for you yet. We'll have the first duck attack then. Who's gonna star?"

We spun it out while he did the blood test. I forced myself to watch him squeeze a drop of blood onto the sensing pad of the tester. "I'm surprised you've got any blood left," I said. "The mosquitoes sucked me dry."

"Yeah, they were rough, weren't they? If I'd thought of it, I could have snared one off my bod and squashed it on this thing. Saved myself a drop of blood." He recorded the number in his notebook. "Yep, going high. Time for a little IJ."

"IJ?"

"Insulin juice. My nickname for it." He rolled a bottle in his palms, drew a dose, and stuck the syringe between his teeth. He slid down his pants a few inches. "You don't have to watch if you don't want to."

"Hey, this is better than a movie. You've got nice legs."

52

"We haven't been out here *that* long. Think about your girl or something."

The girl I hope is still mine, I thought. "I'll try. But you do have nice legs." He snorted and stuck himself under the skin of the thigh. I shivered. "God, that gives me the creeps."

He laughed shortly. "Yeah, me, too. But after a while, it's just something you do without thinking much. A lot of the time, you forget other people are even around." He smiled reflectively. "Last winter, I was sitting in the family room watching TV. Good movie, and I wasn't paying much attention to anything else. I knew it was about time for my shot, so I did the test, got out the IJ, dropped trow, and stuck myself in the butt." He grinned. "And in walks Marcia and a couple of her friends. Should have heard them scream."

I exploded with laughter. "God, you're shitting me?"

"Not an ounce."

"What'd you say?"

"I didn't have time to say anything. They were long gone. Later I sort of apologized to my sister."

"What'd *she* say?"

"Said her friends thought I had cute buns."

"Well, maybe you can get something going there."

"They're a little young. Only eleven or twelve."

"Too bad."

"I guess." He grinned. "Shall we find a campsite?"

"Ready when you are. I thought maybe we'd head for one of those islands."

"Sounds good." He swung his legs around and reached for his paddle. "What's your old man call it when he wants you to paddle?"

"Put the ash to it."

"That's right. What does that mean, anyway?"

"Really good paddles used to be made of ash. He's got a couple over the fireplace at home. But I heard him tell your dad that he thinks these aluminum and plastic jobs are better."

Randy looked at his paddle. "I like the ones with about fifty horsepower that hang on the back of the boat. They get you there a hell of a lot faster with a lot less work."

"Yeah, I like those, too, but they don't let you use motors up here."

"Yeah, no wonder the old guys stayed back on Cant Hook. Well, let's do it."

A chain of small islands stretched in a ragged line toward the faint green of the lake's western shore. The farthest of them seemed to float in the hazy afternoon distance, as much a part of sky as water, and once again I was caught off guard, my mind drifting between shades of blue and green. But maybe here it was okay to drift for a little time while the canoe slid along its silver reflection toward the islands.

We clambered up on the nearest one for a look around. It was high and breezy without a single mosquito or blackfly in residence. People had camped here before, leaving a sapling for hanging packs lashed between a couple of trees and a few charred logs lying in a shallow bowl in the wide granite shelf sloping down to the water.

"What do you think?" I asked.

"Looks fine to me. You build the fire this time, and I'll set up the tent."

I was blowing on the fire, getting a satisfying crackle from the twigs, when he called, "Uh, partner, I think we've got a problem. I got the corners staked down all right, but I'm not hitting anything but rock with the stakes for these ropes."

"Use rocks. Big ones."

"To drive the stakes?"

"No, tie the ropes around them. Just a second and I'll show you." I laid some bigger sticks on the fire and walked over to where he was setting up the tent in the shadow of a boulder the size of a substantial truck.

Anchoring the ropes with rocks was a pretty obvious solution, and he seemed embarrassed. "Well, I guess I would have figured that one out eventually. Old Boy Scout trick?"

"Yeah, we did just about anything we could to get out of the rain."

"Rained a lot, huh?"

"Every damned time. Our scoutmaster had this motto: 'It never rains on Eighty-Nine, it's just a heavy dew.' God, was that a joke. It rained every time we tried to do anything. It was like a curse. Clear blue sky, and we'd just be going for a hike around the block, and *crash*, *boom*, thunder, lightning, monsoon rain the second we stepped out the door. It never failed. My main memory of Boy Scouts is always being soggy." I had him laughing and poured it on. "I mean, it was like some horror movie about living in the jungle. Guys' skin rotted off. They'd take off their boots and they'd have this strange jungle rot on their feet. We used to sit around in the tents at night, trying to figure out what we'd done to get Mother Nature so pissed off. Did you ever read *Lord of the Flies*?"

"Yeah, good book."

"Well, it got kind of like that some of those week-ends. We were ready to sacrifice somebody just to see if we could get a break. Most of the guys thought we might as well start with the scoutmaster, since he was the one with the stupid motto."

"Burn him at the stake?"

I snorted. "You kidding? We couldn't get a fire going in all that rain. We were going to drown him."

"So, did you ever do it?"

"Nah, Dad might have stupid mottoes sometimes, but basically he's a pretty good guy." Randy howled, and I went to check the fire.

We ate freeze-dried beef stew, which was almost as bad as the spaghetti, but we were too hungry to care. Afterward, we sat talking on a granite ledge that jutted high over the lake. Far out on the still water, a pair of loons dove for fish, coming to the surface after what seemed an impossibly long time to cry to each other the news of the world below. After a while, our talk got around to home, and I told him some more about Sonia, admitting that I really was afraid that some other guy would grab her while I was on this stupid trip.

He shrugged. "Well, if she can't wait ten days, maybe she isn't worth worrying about. There are lots of girls in the world."

"Yeah. Trouble is, I've never had a lot of luck with any of them before."

56

"I know that problem. I freeze up when it comes to small talk. I mean, once you're done talking about school and movies and music, what the hell do you say? I never know."

"That's part of the reason I like Sonia; she does most of the talking."

"Well, you tell good stories. I've never had any luck making girls laugh. But, don't worry, I'm working on some killer diabetes stories." He got to his feet. "And speaking of the Big D, I've got to check my blood."

He was back in a minute with his kit and went through the usual routine. While he was finding the right page in his notebook, I asked, "Could I have a closer look at the ol' Glucotron?"

"Sure, but you don't have a hair on your ass if you don't let me test your blood."

"No way."

"Wimp."

"Oh, hell. Okay, go ahead." I closed my eyes and stuck out a finger as he cocked the needle gizmo.

"Got to watch."

"I watch you, that's enough. Come on, get it over with — Ouch! Shit, that hurts!"

He squeezed my finger. "Steady. I've got to get a drop of blood. There."

I sucked on my finger. "How many times a day do you have to do that?"

"Only four. The rest of the time I just do it for fun." He waited a moment for the reading on the Glucotron. "You're normal. Lucky bastard. No IJ for you."

He cleaned the tester and needle gizmo with an

alcohol wipe and stuck them back in his kit. "What's IJ actually do for you?" I asked.

"Didn't your dad tell you all the gruesome details?"

"Some, but I didn't pay a lot of attention. Now I'm interested."

He shrugged. "Well, it's pretty simple, really. Insulin's a hormone that lets cells absorb sugar. Your body produces it, mine doesn't. Or at least not enough of it. So, I have to give myself insulin out of a bottle. All the testing is to make sure I keep my blood sugar at the right level. Not enough sugar and I need something high energy. Too much, and I need to give myself some IJ so my cells can absorb the extra. It's all a matter of keeping things in balance."

"And if you don't?"

"Well, if I go way high or way low for too long, I'll pass out."

"Uh, should I know what to do if that happens?"

"It's not going to happen. I've had the Big D for almost five years, and I've never passed out. Don't worry about it."

I shrugged. "Okay. I just thought I ought to know."

He sighed. "Look, I'll tell you a quick story if we can talk about something else after that."

"Only if it's a good story."

"Oh, it's a real thigh-slapper. About a year ago, I had a crush on this girl named Roxanne. Now most of my friends have seen me test my blood and give myself a shot. But Roxanne was new in school. Anyway, a bunch of us were over at the roller rink on a Saturday morning, and she saw me pop myself with some IJ. And she just flipped. Jumped up and ran to the bathroom. This girl I've known for a long time went after her and explained everything, but Roxanne won't come near me after that. Looked at me like I was some kind of freak."

"Real nice girl."

"Yeah. Well, some people react funny. Anyway, I was pretty damned embarrassed, and when I went home that noon, I said to hell with it. No more testing, no more IJ, no more giving in to the Big D. So I shoved my kit in the bottom of my dresser and went down to Mac's, where I did a major binge on everything I'm supposed to watch. I skipped my testing that afternoon, did another pig-out at supper, and then skipped my usual evening shot. And I felt great. Just fine. Until about eleven that night when my brain decided to go into a major fade. Mom and Dad were out, and Marcia and I were watching the late movie. And I knew what was going on: I needed IJ and I needed it bad because I had pushed my sugar way, way high. But it seemed too much trouble to do anything about it. So I just sat there, even though I couldn't follow the movie anymore or think a single intelligent thought. Finally Marcia looked at me, and she got real scared because it was real obvious that I was not doing worth a crap. And it was seeing that look on her face that finally made me move, but she had to help me find my kit and get out the IJ."

"And you were okay after you had your shot?"

"Yeah. I didn't feel real good because I'd really done the sugar thing, but my brain started working again. Anyway, that was the first and only time I ever tried to push the Big D around. Now I just ride it. And I don't fall off, so don't mother-hen me, man. Because that really pisses me off."

I held up my palms. "You're the expert. I am definitely okay with that."

"Good. Let's talk about something else."

For a few minutes, we watched the sunset turning the water and the sky a deep gold. "How come we haven't seen anybody else?" he asked.

"It's getting kind of late in the season, and we're not on one of the popular routes. The old guys chose it so we'd really be off on our own."

"Well, they chose right, I guess." He shivered. "Brrr, it's getting cool. Time to build up the fire and make something hot to drink."

I hesitated, feeling that I should say something after all he'd told me. "Uh, maybe they'll find a cure one of these days."

"Are you still thinking about that crap? Forget it. The Big D ain't so bad once you get used to it. If they find a cure, great. Otherwise, I'll just have to enjoy the Big D as long as I can."

"What's to enjoy?"

"I'm working on that. You get the fire going, and I'll dig around for some cocoa."

CHAPTER FOUR

I squinted at the ray of sunlight coming through the tent flap. What the hell time was it, anyway? I dug around in my clothes and found my watch. Quarter of six? I hadn't been up this early in my life! And I wasn't planning to start. I gave Randy's feet a kick to chase them back to his side of the tent, curled up, and closed my eyes. But I didn't feel like sleeping, which meant, of course, that it must be more like quarter of eleven. I found my watch again, opened my eyes a little wider, and read it again. Ten of six. I'll be damned.

I bundled up my clothes and slipped out of the tent. I stood, the pine needles prickly under my bare feet, and had a look at the morning. Over the lake, half a dozen gulls tilted on the breeze, white on the blue of water and cloudless sky. Nice, almost worth painting a picture. I walked barefoot past the remains of our fire and up onto the granite ledge overlooking the lake. I sat there for a few minutes, my eyes half closed, letting the breeze wash the colors over me.

A silly idea started forming in my head, and I looked down into the water. God, it'd be colder than hell. But

I felt grubby, my face oily from the night's sleep and my body itchy with the dirt and dried sweat of the hard passage across the swampy lakes. Was I really stupid enough to do this? I went to get soap and a towel.

The lip of the ledge was a good ten feet above the lake, but the rock beveled in below and then out again to a shelf just above the water. I made my way carefully down to the shelf, stripped off my shorts and T-shirt, and stood poised on the edge. This was going to hurt. I took a deep breath and jumped.

Ever see pictures of those idiots who belong to polar bear clubs? Well, believe me, those guys don't know what cold is. I came to the surface yelping like an otter with his nuts caught in a trap. For maybe a minute, all I could do was thrash around chattering curses. Then the cold seemed to go away, leaving me strangely warm. It's hypothermia, I thought, the next stage is probably paralysis, followed shortly by death. But my arms and legs still worked, and I swam out toward the sunlight beyond the shadow of the ledge. The rays slanted deep, and I dove, following the light down to the white sand, touched, and kicked up through the light to break water in the sun again.

"You are definitely shitting me." Randy stood on the ledge, watching me. "If your girl could just see you now, skinny-dipping in the wilderness just like Huck Finn."

"Yeah, she'd be impressed, huh? Come on in, it's great."

"I've got to have something to eat." He turned away.

"You don't have a hair on your ass if you don't do it," I called after him.

"I'll see if I can find any stupid pills in the first-aid kit. Then maybe I'll think about it."

I swam back to the shelf, hoisted myself up, soaped down, and slipped back in. I'd just gotten the suds out of my hair when I heard a splash. A moment later, Randy shot to the surface. "Holy shit," he yelled. "That's cold!"

"It gets better. Just tread water for a minute."

He splashed about, yelping. "God, where's the soap? I can't stand this."

"Over on the shelf. But you still don't have a hair on your ass if you don't swim out a ways."

"Then I don't have a hair on my ass. All I wanta do is get clean and get out."

We lay naked on the ledge, watching the gulls and letting the sun dry us. "I thought you didn't like the water," Randy said. "Your dad told mine that you're afraid of it."

"Nice of him to pass that on."

Randy shrugged. "Well, they're brothers, and I think they talk a lot about us. Sometimes I wish I had a brother."

"I've got two; they're overrated." I turned on my back. "No, I don't like the water much. Never have. Don't you remember at Maple Grove when you, Bob, and your mom used to swim out to the raft without me? I hated that."

He frowned. "I remember swimming out to the raft,

but I don't remember that it was any big deal that you didn't."

"Well, it was to me. Something else I wasn't any good at."

"You swim pretty well now."

"I don't sink, but that's only because Mom and Dad made me go through beginners swimming about six times. And when that didn't work, they turned me over to Bob."

"The Nazi? I'll bet that was a treat."

"Sure was. Bob and his swim-team buddies used to do laps in the high school pool before school, and he dragged me along. I don't think he figured it'd take him more than a day or two to get my ass straightened out, but I had him fooled on that one."

"Contrary, huh?"

"I guess so. His theory was to push me out just past where I could touch and then to keep shoving me back every time I tried to get by him into the shallow end. Which meant I was always somewhere between drowning and getting my feet on the bottom so I could get my head above water."

"Or swimming."

"I didn't see it that way. Anyway, I'd cry and try to push around him and he'd push me back. Then I'd try to hit him and he'd dunk me good and then we'd go through the routine again. About the third day, I bit him and he swatted me a hard one. I really started crying then, and that's when Pete saved me."

"Pete, the Mountain Man?"

"The same. He told Bob to take a break, got an arm across my chest, and just towed me around until I calmed down. Then he started working with me while Bob did some laps. And because I didn't want to go through that crap with Bob ever again, I swam, man. Right then and there, I swam."

"Not right away? Come on, nobody learns that fast."

"Oh, I'm not saying I was ready for the team. But remember, I'd been through all those swimming classes, and this time I was trying like hell. And Pete was right alongside of me, telling me how I was getting it and laughing and reaching out to give me a boost or what he called a 'shark bite.' And I kept swimming."

"Pissed off Bob, I'll bet."

"You got that. Bob never liked getting shown up at anything. But Pete put him off when he tried to take over again. Later, they must have had it out, because the next day Bob didn't say a word, just went to do his laps. After a week working with Pete, I was getting along okay without him or Bob or anybody."

"The Mountain Man sounds like kind of a neat guy."

"Yeah, he is. But even he couldn't make me *like* the water. Voluntarily, I spend about two minutes in the shower every morning. Otherwise, I leave it alone."

"Then explain to me what you were doing out there this morning."

I shrugged and reached for my clothes. "I think the BO started to poison my brain. It was get clean or die. Hey, I'm hungry. What'd you eat?"

"Just a granola bar. I knew I had to get in the water or listen to you bragging all day and complaining about how I smelled. So I wanted to get it over with quick." He started pulling on his clothes. "By the way, what are we going to do today?"

"I guess we're supposed to be up here fishing. Want to give it a try?"

"I don't give a damn about the fishing, but I wouldn't mind eating some fish instead of that freeze-dried crap."

"Okay. Let's see if we can catch something."

We ate a cold breakfast and then got out the small tackle box, the net, and the pair of lightweight rods Dad had packed for us. We spread the stuff out on the ledge and managed to assemble the rods. I tied a vicious-looking lure to Randy's line and handed the pole to him. He flexed it experimentally and then swung it back for a cast. "Hold on," I said. "Better let me show you how. Dad's got a lot of nasty stories about digging hooks out of people's necks and ears."

"Okay, Joe Nature. Teach me angling."

Not an easy trick when I knew damned little about it myself. I stood. "Okay, first you hold down the button on the reel . . . ."

We practiced casting for half an hour and then loaded our gear and some lunch in the canoe. We worked our way west through the islands, fishing the shorelines and then crossing the open water under a sky as high and blue as any I'd ever seen. We weren't catching anything, but the sun was warm enough for us to take off our shirts and every island gave us something new to see.

About noon, we were skirting a long, flat island. A band of crows had taken up residence in a half dozen dead trees on the eastern tip, and I paused to watch them swaying and cawing on the high branches. "You know," I said, "I heard those darned things can live as long as a human being. Even longer."

Randy looked up from cleaning weeds off his lure. "No fooling? I didn't know any birds lived that long."

"Well, I guess I'd have to look it up to be sure, but that's what I remember hearing. I'm hungry. Want a sandwich?"

"Sure."

I shipped my paddle and started digging into the lunch. "I think we picked the best island," I said. "They all look nice, but I haven't seen any as nice as ours."

Randy cast lazily toward shore again and started reeling in without paying much attention to his lure skimming just below the surface. "Yeah, I think we made a pretty good — " A sudden jerk on the line nearly yanked the pole from his hands. "Hey, I think I've got a bite! Wait a second, I'm not sure now. I thought — " A fish broke water in a rush, snapping silver in the air as it tried to throw the bait. Randy pulled back hard, and the lure tore out of its mouth, zinging over the canoe to land on the other side. "Damn," he said.

"Jeez, take it easy with that thing. I think the hooks parted my hair."

"Sorry. I guess I was supposed to play it some, huh? Kind of tire it out?"

"Something like that."

"What kind of fish was it, anyway?"

"I'm not sure, but it looked a little like the bass Dad's got mounted in the rec room at home."

"Well, at least there are fish in here. I was beginning to have my doubts. Let's get closer and try again."

We paddled in, lunch forgotten and both suddenly interested in what we'd never given a damn about before. Randy got another bite almost immediately and managed to bring the fish close enough to the canoe for me to net. I held it up for him to see. "Hey, will you look at that," he said. "That's plenty big enough to eat, isn't it?"

"Yeah, it's a pretty nice fish. Not any kind of champion, but big enough to fillet." I got a good grip on the bass and started working the treblehook out of its mouth. "Now don't jerk that lure," I said. "I've got my fingers on the hooks."

"Trust me. I'm a pro, now."

"You wish. There." I tossed the lure back in the water and got out the stringer, trying to picture how Dad pushed the sharp point through a fish's mouth and out its gills. Or was it the other way around? I thought, decided to start from the mouth side, and managed to get the point through the gills on the third try. I tied the other end of the stringer to my seat and lowered the fish overboard. It flopped a couple of times, splashing me, and then settled down, its tail waving disconsolately.

"Suppose a bigger fish comes along and swallows it?" Randy said.

"Then I guess we'll have a lot bigger fish to eat." I threw my lure toward the shore.

A couple of minutes later, I caught a bass a little smaller than Randy's. Before I could get it on the stringer, Randy had his second, and it was a beauty. "It's all in the wrists," he chortled.

"Right," I grumped, managing to net it one-handed.

I got mine on the stringer and then started working on his. It was hooked hard, and I had to dig to get the lure free. I'd about gotten it out when the fish decided to give a mighty thrash. I jerked my right hand clear of the hooks but lost hold with my left. The lure went sailing as the fish hit the water with a plop and was gone. "You threw back my fish!" Randy yelped.

I examined the tip of my forefinger to see if the barb of the hook had drawn blood. It hadn't. "Well, not intentionally."

He looked forlornly into the water. "That was my best fish."

"Oh, stop whining," I said. "You'll get another."

"You'd better hope so," he said. "Right now, you're the one who's going to eat that freeze-dried crap if we don't have enough fish for two."

"Give me a break."

He grinned. "Oh, all right. Let's eat some lunch and then try the other side of the island."

"I need to get out for a while. Let's go up on shore."

We ate at the edge of the narrow beach and then settled back against a couple of cedar trees. I felt lazy and wouldn't have minded a half-hour siesta, but Randy was feeling talkative. "You know," he said, "I'm beginning to think that the Indians had it pretty good back before Columbus. Living here would beat sitting around Europe waiting to catch the plague or something."

"Real cold in the winter," I said. "And not a lot to do."

"You could always take the dogsled into town once

a week. Catch a few beers and a movie, stay overnight in a motel with a heated pool. Not a bad life, if you ask me."

I tilted my hat back to look at him. "You know, you really do have a very strange sense of humor."

He laughed. "Just sometimes. What kind of Indians would be up here, anyway?"

"Chippewa, I think."

"You got any Indians in your school?"

"Quite a few. There are more Indians in Minneapolis than just about any other city in the country, I think."

"We had nine or ten in my school last year as part of some kind of government program. Magnet school stuff. They were real quiet, real hard to get to know."

"Well, we haven't exactly given them a lot of reason to trust us."

"Yeah, but it's not like I was buddies with Custer. I'm willing to start over."

"Maybe you are, but I'm not sure they are."

"Well, maybe not. Still, I think I'm gonna try harder to get to know some of them next year. . . . So, do you want to catch some fish?"

"Might as well. I wanted to take a nap, but it doesn't look like you're going to shut up any time soon."

"Hey, if you'd said — "

"Forget it. I'm just giving you a hard time. Come on, let's go catch supper."

In the next couple of hours, we didn't land anything big enough to keep, but we covered a lot of water and a lot about our lives. He got mostly A's and B's, wrote for the school newspaper, played tennis on the JV team, and actually enjoyed practicing the piano. All of which didn't do wonders for my ego, since lately I'd gotten more D's than C's, never wrote more than my name if I could avoid it, hadn't made the first cut when I tried out for football, and had bombed in one year of playing the trumpet. Needless to say, I kept my answers short.

Eventually, he noticed and turned in his seat. "Uh, am I talking too much?"

I shrugged. "I guess not. I'm just kind of surprised. You're not usually this talkative."

He looked embarrassed. "Yeah, I guess you're right. It's just . . ." He waved a hand at the water and the sky. "I don't know. I'm just really enjoying all this."

And I was, too. Strange. "Well, go ahead and talk. I don't mind."

We were passing a tiny island, little more than a sharp-sided boulder, topped by three or four scraggly spruce trees. Randy cast toward the shore, snapping the pole back so that the lure dropped neatly into the shadow of the rock. You show-off, I thought, and tried the same trick. But I put too much muscle into it, jerked back too late, and watched helplessly as my lure whipped twice around an overhanging branch. "Oh, shit," I said.

Randy turned on his imitation of Dad. "Look, son, trick is you've got to — "

"Stick it, Charlie."

He laughed and reeled in his lure. "Come on. Paddle us close and I'll get it. Hand me your pole."

I did, and he reeled in as I paddled. When the bow nudged the rock, he stood and worked the tip of the pole back and forth until the lure broke free. "There. No damage done," he said.

71

"Thanks," I said sourly, and took my pole back. Crap. In another day or two, he'd know how to do everything better than I did.

Randy ran his hand down the side of the broken rock. "You know, we studied some geology in science last year. I think this is part of what's called the Canadian Shield."

"Oh, wow. What the hell's the Canadian Shield?"

He ignored the sarcasm. "This big layer of bedrock from Lake Superior back across most of western Canada. I remember my teacher saying . . ."

I stopped listening, my eye suddenly caught by a strange play of color in the moss growing in the thin soil on the sloping side of the rock. I leaned one way and then the other, watching the specks of red, yellow, and silver change pattern against the green moss. Weird. And very nice. I leaned closer, studying. The reds and the yellows were tiny flowers. I wasn't sure about the silvers. I sat back and let my mind frame it, imagining how I'd set the moss in the upper left-hand quadrant and then let it fall across the picture, like a waterfall of color against the fissured black of the granite. . . . I would, that is, if I could ever make my fingers paint anything close to what I could imagine. But I couldn't, of course, so screw it.

". . . Anyway, that Precambrian granite is about the oldest rock in the earth's crust," Randy finished. He looked at me, expecting some applause for the lecture, I guess. I didn't give him any. He hesitated. "So," he said, "do you like science?"

"No, I think it's boring as hell."

"Oh . . . Well, uh, what do you like?"

"I liked recess, but they don't give us that anymore. Come on, let's get going."

We paddled on toward the last island in the chain. "So, you don't like any of your classes?" he asked.

God, couldn't he just leave it alone? "No, not much. Just imagine trying to follow someone like Bob through school. Every teacher who ever had him expects me to be just like him: brain, jock, president of this, captain of that. But I get them over that quick. I'm not my big brother, and I don't want to be."

"Ah, the middle-child number again. You ought to quit that."

"Hey, I would if I could, man," I snapped. "You want a big brother? You can have Bob. Anytime."

"No, thanks."

"Well, then lay off the middle-child crap. It's not an excuse, it's the way things are."

"Hey, don't get pissed. I was just razzing you. I'm sure it's a bitch trying to follow him. But, just for the record, I'm glad I'm doing this trip with you, not Bob the Nazi."

I spent a long minute gazing across the lake at the hazy outline of the western shore. A breeze from the south rippled over the water, silvering the surface for just a moment before it slid past us on its way north. And I wondered how we'd gotten arguing and started ruining the afternoon. "Yeah, me, too," I said. "We're doin' okay together. . . . But, you know, we're not accomplishing crap on this fishing number."

"That bay over there looks like a likely spot."

"How would you know?"

"It's simple. You see how that granite ledge slopes

down from the shore, that means that under the water — "

"Stop bullshitting me."

He laughed. "Well, it was sounding pretty good."

"You can't fool Joe Nature or his big mama."

"Mother Nature?"

"You got it, Charlie. Are you gonna paddle or talk all day?"

We pushed into the bay almost to the shore but didn't get any bites. "No luck here," Randy said. "What do we do now that we've run out of islands?"

I glanced at the sun. "We've got plenty of time to take a look at the far shore. Maybe we'll catch something over there."

"Well, as long as you can find our way back home, I'm willing."

"Okay, I said, "let me get *das Boot* turned around."

"Ah, *der Junge spricht Deutsch*. Must be *der nazi Bruder's* influence."

"Just help me keep it from running aground, huh?"

Outside the bay, he asked, "So you had some German, huh?"

"Just a year. I wasn't any good at that, either."

"There you go running yourself down again."

I grunted. Yeah, but at least I was truthful.

We crossed the open water, reaching the western shore a couple of miles north of the portage we'd take to Talking Bird Lake when we started the trip back to the resort and civilization. I showed Randy the spot on the map. "Let's go north a ways," I said. "We'll see the shore to the south in a couple of days."

"Suits me. Just as long as we catch fish."

We paddled along the shore, pausing to cast into the shallows. And for reasons known only to fish and perhaps to people who actually knew something about fishing, we started getting bites. Randy landed two walleyes, while I caught a walleye and two bass. My walleye was the nicest fish of the day, and I held it up to show him.

"Nice fish," he said. "Just about as nice as the one you lost of mine."

"The hell. This one's twice as big."

He squinted. "Could be an inch longer, I guess."

"Well, we've each caught four, so we're even for the day. Let's head back."

"Hey, don't forget you lost one of mine."

"Yeah, that's right. Okay, you're one behind."

"No, your math's screwed up. You lost one of mine, so you're penalized two, which puts me two ahead."

"One," I said.

"Okay, have it your way. I'm one ahead, you lose." He grinned his I-gotcha smirk.

"I think I've been fished," I said.

"Looks like. Speaking of which, what are we going to do with all these fish?"

"Well, we can't eat all of them tonight, that's for sure."

"Could we keep the rest on the stringer overnight?"

"I guess, but did you feel how much just those two slowed us down on the way over here? Seven will be like towing a concrete block. Let's just take what we need for tonight and let the rest go."

"Okay by me. But I need to take a whiz. Let's land over by that little stream."

I put my walleye in the bottom of the canoe, where it flopped angrily while we paddled into the shallow inlet where a stream flowed across a strip of sand beach and into the lake. Randy climbed out and pulled the bow up a foot onto the sand. "Coming?" he asked.

"No, I'm fine. I'm going to deal with these fish."

Sorting through a stringer of flopping bass and wall-eyes is not the easiest trick in the world, but I was making progress when Randy strolled back from the brush. He perched his rump on the bow, and started offering advice on the selection. "Randy, if you don't want to swallow one of these fish whole, shut up."

He laughed. "Sure, boss."

"And don't start that again." I leaned over the side to release the smallest of the bass.

I'd watched Dad lower fish into the water, cradling them gently in a big hand until they got the idea that they were free again. I did the same with the three smallest fish from our stringer. They swam off, apparently none the worse for wear. "You'd think they'd be a little happier about it," Randy said. "You know, leap, dive, cavort a little."

"They're not dolphins," I said. "They're fish, which makes them stone stupid." I retied the stringer and lowered the four fish doomed to be our supper into the lake to trail behind us as we paddled home. "Well, I'm ready," I said. "Cast off all lines."

"Aye, aye, captain," Randy said. He put one foot in the canoe and pushed off with the other, swiveling to take his seat as we glided free of the shore. I swung the bow as he hit one, two, three strokes, and we were pointed out of the inlet just as graceful as you please — like we'd been raised doing this and were as comfortable as a pair of young Chippewa braves in a canoe on water.

Ever notice how reality has a habit of jerking your chain just about the time you're feeling comfortable? At that moment, we heard a grunt and a crash in the brush to our left, and a bear about the size of a Honda sauntered out of the woods. "A bear," Randy yelped.

"I know it's a bear!" I backwatered furiously, rammed the shore with the stern, had an image of the bear taking a seat in the canoe, and started paddling hard in the other direction. But there wasn't any escape that way, either, since the bear only needed to take about three bounds to be standing in the mouth of the inlet waiting for us. Could bears bound? Hell, I didn't know. But I wasn't about to take a chance with this one, who looked suspiciously agile. I stopped, the paddle frozen in my hands.

"What do we do now?" Randy hissed.

"Just don't make any sudden movements and let me think."

Having enjoyed the effect of his entrance, the bear flopped down on his rump to study us in detail.

"You still thinking?" Randy whispered.

"I'm thinking maybe we ought to wait until he leaves."

"Is that the best you can do?"

"You got a better idea?"

We sat rock still for maybe five minutes while the bear stared at us. "He doesn't seem in any hurry to leave," Randy whispered.

"No . . . Maybe we could edge along the opposite shore until we're past him."

"Suppose he doesn't like that?"

"I don't think they attack," I said, wishing I had real proof of that. "Dad said they're just your ordinary, everyday black bears."

"Yeah, but he's not out here discussing transit rights with one of them. Maybe we ought to throw him the fish."

"I'm not going to throw him our fish! We worked hard for that meal."

"Yeah, but — "

The bear got up just then, lifted his nose to sniff the air, and sauntered down the beach. I took a couple of strokes as quietly as I could to keep our distance from him. "Get ready," I whispered. "We'll make a run for it in a second."

"Hold on, I think he's about to get distracted." The bear paused to nose around a fallen tree, then lifted a huge paw and tore away a couple of feet of bark. "Looking for bugs or worms," Randy said. "I saw a nature program — "

"Save the lecture for later. Just let him do his thing."

The bear started lapping at something with his long purplish tongue. "Mmmm, good," Randy said.

"Okay," I said. "Ready, *go!*"

We hydroplaned through the mouth of the inlet. The bear raised his head to gaze curiously after us, and then went back to his snack. When we were well clear, we rested panting on our paddles and watched him demolish the log. Finally, when he'd eaten what he wanted, he turned his broad rump to us, backed up a couple of steps, and then moseyed into the brush.

"I guess he wasn't all that interested in us, after all," Randy said.

"Just a couple of city kids in a canoe. Not a big deal."

"Yeah. But unless I'm imagining things, he mooned us before he left."

"I got that feeling, too. Well, I'm sure glad we're not camping over here."

"No shit. That thing was big. How well can they swim, anyway?"

"I'm not sure, but I think we're pretty safe on the island. That's a long way from shore."

"Maybe, but I'll tell you one thing; I'm going to hang that food pack a little higher tonight."

"Yeah, that'd probably be a good idea."

We'd gone a long way, and it took us until nearly dusk to get back. After all the sun, the paddling, and the bear, our island looked damned good. And even though I knew I'd never try to paint the picture, I rested on my paddle a moment, wanting to remember how our island looked with its reflection traced in gold as the sunset washed the horizon behind us.

"Nice," Randy said. "Good to be home."

"Yeah. Real good."

He glanced at his watch. "Partner, I don't mean to hurry you, but I should have eaten an hour ago. I want to get something in my stomach before I start feeling like crap."

"Okay. Let's go cook some fish."

I wasn't exactly an expert, but I managed to clean and fillet the fish while Randy got the fire going. We boiled some dehydrated potatoes and onions and then fried them with the fillets. The potatoes and onions were pretty chewy, but the fish was great.

When we couldn't eat any more, we built up the fire, and settled ourselves on the ledge as the stars began coming out.

"What do you suppose Bob and the Mountain Man did after supper?" Randy asked.

I shrugged. "Probably planned their lives. The details, anyway."

"Did Bob want to be in the army back then?"

"Oh, yeah. He's wanted to be an army officer as long as I can remember. He'll probably be a general someday. Hell, he's already racking up points."

"And your folks think you should be just like him?"

God, I didn't want to get into this. "No, not just like him. I don't think they're stupid enough to think I'm cut out for the army. But they'd like me to do something right."

"Like what?"

"Well, for starters, they're not real thrilled that their darling boy ain't done for shit in school recently. My grades are lousy, I'm a wash at sports, and I don't do music, drama, or anything else."

"Uh, no offense, but what *do* you do?"

"I just try to get by without causing anybody any trouble. So, I just hang out, man. But they're not exactly charmed with most of the people I hang out with, including Sonia."

"What's wrong with Sonia?"

"Nothing's wrong with Sonia. Hell, Dad's never even met her and Mom's only met her once. And that was for about five minutes at the mall."

"Must not have gone well."

"Went fine from everything I could tell, but when I got home Mom called her a 'mall lizard' and said I could do better."

"*Mall lizard*? Where in hell did she get that?"

"I don't know. Maybe she made it up. Dad said it wasn't accurate because it was a takeoff on lounge lizard, and that's a male term. And Mom got really pissed and said that she didn't 'give a capital *D-A-M-N*' whether it was male or female, but that he ought to stop playing the picky engineer and have a talk with me about appropriate girls."

"Whoa. Sounds like Sonia made a big impression. What did she do to win your mama's heart?"

"I don't know what she did. Maybe it was something about how she was dressed."

"Like all the other mall lizards?"

I glared at him, but he gave me his complete-innocence look, which almost made me laugh. "I guess. It's not like she dresses real down or anything, but she's got this old brown leather jacket — you know, a bomber jacket — and her hair's got kind of the *mall-lizard* look. And get this, she pops her gum."

"Oh, my God. Well, I certainly see your mother's point: This girl is definitely not appropriate." He started giggling.

"I mean, can you believe that Mom actually made a big deal out of that? Said that she thought Sonia could

81

at least stop popping her gum long enough to be polite."

We were both giggling now. "So," Randy choked, "they sent you up here to keep you out of the clutches of a leather-jacketed, mother-insulting, gum-popping *mall lizard*?" We exploded with laughter.

When I finally got control again, I said, "All I know is that Mom was a lot more enthusiastic about this trip after she met Sonia."

"Meanwhile what'd your dad have to say about 'appropriate girls'?"

"Oh, that part was kind of disappointing. He just explained how every mother wants her son to find a woman who'll settle him down, point him in the right direction, and keep him in line while he earns a good living, goes to church, fathers grandkids, and makes his mother proud."

"Fathers grandkids? Isn't it a little early for that?"

"That's exactly what I asked, and he got kind of red and said that he was talking about 'the long view' and that starting off all mothers want their sons to date wholesome girls with 'modest' figures."

"Okay, now we're getting to the exciting part: T and A, one of my favorite subjects."

"Mine, too. I asked what he meant by 'modest' and he laughed and said that no mother wants her son to date a girl with a bigger bust than she has."

Randy laughed. "I didn't know that. How does Sonia, uh, stack up?"

"Mom's got a problem," I said. "A sizable one."

"So what'd he say next?"

"I think he was kind of shocked that he'd said that

much, so he just asked if I had any questions. I didn't."

"You should have asked him how he felt about wholesome girls with modest figures when he was a teenager."

"I felt like it, but I figured the less said, the less grief I was going to get about Sonia."

Randy lay back chuckling. "God, that bust thing is funny. And I'll bet you it's true, too."

"Yeah, I think it is."

"Oh, you devious mothers. Got to watch 'em."

"That's for sure." We lay for a few minutes, gazing at the stars. "You know," I said, "I was really pissed at Mom and Dad for a lot of things this summer. Especially making me go on this trip. But I'm glad we came. A lot of that stuff doesn't seem very important now."

"I know what you mean. . . . Hey, do you remember that time we got everybody hyper-pissed at us? You know, that afternoon we left the resort and went into the village by ourselves?"

"Oh, I remember that real well. We walked through the woods to the old cemetery and then down the road to that old country store right at the edge of Maynard."

"Uh-huh. We'd done it before with grown-ups or Bob, and I guess we figured it wasn't a big deal if we went on our own."

"Sure. It was a hot day, we needed a pop, and we knew the way. Why not?" I smiled, picturing again that afternoon when the sun burned a perfect sulfur yellow in a sky as blue as forever, while the two of us, nine years old and too young to worry a lot, made our way through the pine woods to the crooked wrought-iron fence, where we — but not grown-ups or even Bob — could slip through a narrow break into the old cemetery. And then, because this time there was no one to hurry us along, we took our time kicking through the tall weeds and scrambling over the tilting gravestones of people so long dead that no one bothered to cut the grass but once or twice a summer.

"Did that cemetery scare you?" I asked without opening my eyes.

"No, and that's kind of funny, because I remember some others did. How about you?"

"No, that was a friendly place. The people had been dead too long to worry about. The only thing that scared me was walking on the side of the road until we got to the store."

"That scared me, too, but it was worth it. God, that store was a great place. Must have been there a century."

"Under one owner, too. You remember her?"

"Mrs. Ludwig? God, who could forget her? She had that big goiter on her neck and that long gray braid and she was always popping her false teeth."

"And she didn't like kids. Watched us every second we were in the place."

"You know, I think we would've been okay if we'd just had our pop and then beaten it home. It was your idea of having a picnic in the cemetery that did us in."

"My idea, huh?"

"As I recall."

"You recall wrong. It was your idea as much as mine."

"Could be, I guess. But we were pretty dumb. We didn't even catch on that we were in for it when we heard the bell ringing at the resort and people shouting in the woods. We just thought it was time for supper. Boy, the moms and the dads were pissed when they found us."

"Uh-huh. But you know who was the most pissed? Bob. They made him look after us all the rest of the week." I hesitated. "You know, he must have been about the same age we are now. I never thought of that before."

"He sure seemed a lot older. Hey, you aren't starting to sympathize with him, are you?"

"Not a chance."

"Yeah, once a Nazi always a Nazi. But, you know, even with everybody pissed at us, the whole thing was worth it. Every time I think about the good times we had at those reunions, that's the day I always remember."

"Yeah, me too."

Neither of us said anything for a few minutes as the fire burned down and far across the lake a loon cried. "You know," Randy said, "we were really buddies back then. I missed that after Grandpa died and we stopped going to Winona."

"Yeah, I missed that, too. . . . Hey, I'm bushed. Maybe we ought to hang the food pack and call it a night."

"Oh, hell. I forgot about the damned food pack. What do you say we just close it up tight and forget about it tonight? You said it, no bear's going to swim out this far."

"Yeah, but a squirrel or a chipmunk could get in it."

"A squirrel'll get in it even if we've got it hanging."

"Maybe not as easy. Come on, let's not take a chance."

"Oh, all right. I'll lift, you pull on the rope."

CHAPTER
FIVE

I was still half asleep when Randy whispered, "Mark?"

"What is it?" I mumbled.

"Last one in has no hair on his ass." He scrambled for the door. I lunged, catching him by an ankle before he got through. But he was pretty slick for a runt, rolling to break my grip and then jerking the pole up so that the tent collapsed on me. That slowed me for a few seconds and he was halfway to the lake before I was untangled and sprinting after him. There was only one way I was going to beat him, and I never even thought twice. I pulled off my sweatshirt, threw it aside, and took the high road. Randy was still scrambling down the rock to the shelf just above the water when I hit the lip of the ledge and launched myself out over the ten-foot drop.

Between the time my feet left the ledge and I hit the water, I had time to consider several important questions: What kind of day was it? Nice. Maybe even a little bit warmer than yesterday. Was there anything below me except very cold water? Nope, nobody'd moved any rocks during the night and no bears or moose were swimming by at the moment. Was Randy impressed with my machismo? Seemed to be. His jaw was hanging open, anyway. Was it going to hurt more if I folded into a cannonball or went in feetfirst? God knows, it was going to hurt plenty either way, but feetfirst seemed a slightly less painful option. Which brought me to the final question: What the hell was I doing? I was scared of the water. Really and truly. I was scared now. Very. It was going to be wet. And cold. Very damned —

I hit, the impact and the cold shutting down all brain activity and most other body functions as well. Maybe I actually blacked out, because I hardly remember being under water before I popped to the surface and started treading water frantically while my teeth rattled like berserk castanets.

"You win," Randy said from the shelf. "You've got by far the hairiest ass."

" 'Bout time you admitted it," I chattered.

"No argument. But, tell me, what did you yell when you jumped? It was one awesome noise."

"Uh, 'Geronimo,' I think."

"Hmmm. Sounded more like wordless terror to me."

"Maybe that was it. You getting in or not?"

"Don't rush me. I'm just gonna ease into this."

We swam for half an hour and then got ourselves some breakfast. "Today, I'm going to catch the big one," Randy said.

"Second day of fishing, and he's already making promises."

"You just watch. I've got a feeling about it. You about ready? The fish bite better before it's too hot."

"Do they really?" I said sarcastically.

"Yep. Come on."

We fished the shores of a couple of small islands to the northeast on the edge of the chain and then set off across open water toward a large island to the north. Beyond it, Ax Handle stretched nearly out of sight, and only by squinting could I make out the faintest outline of the north shore.

We had a nice southwesterly breeze that boosted us along, and we had the leisure to talk as we paddled. Today, I'd be damned if I'd let Randy quiz me about all the stupid crap going on in my life. So before he could start, I asked him if he'd gotten to any Cardinals games and whether he thought St. Louis had a shot at the pennant.

We spent a safe hour on baseball and were nearly to the big island before the subject began petering out. I cast about for another question. "So, do you all go to the games? Or just you and your dad?"

"Marcia comes along a lot of the time."

"How about your mom?"

He snorted. "*The Mom?* Shit. *The Mom* doesn't have time for stuff like that. When Marcia turned eight, *the Mom* went back to work full time, and for her that means about sixteen hours a day. We haven't seen a lot of her since. But I don't figure she'll stick around much longer, anyway."

"Whoa. Come again?"

"Oh, *the Mom* and Dad are just making a show of it these days, and not doing a very good job of it, either. They don't talk, they don't sleep in the same bed, and we haven't gone anywhere as a family in a couple of years."

"What happened?"

He shrugged. "They're just not in the same zone anymore. I mean, my dad's a heck of a salesman. He knows everything there is to know about copiers and fax machines. But he's still just a salesman, while *she* is St. Louis's hotshot female lawyer these days. And that's a big zone difference, man. She's designer clothes and champagne, he's still blue jeans and beer."

"Sounds like a country-and-western song," I said.

"Yeah. And just about as depressing. But don't get me wrong. I'm proud as hell of her. She's made herself into somebody. And it's not that she doesn't try to do the good-parenting number. After she wins a big case, she always brings home a video and a pizza, or maybe Chinese food. She'll hug Marcia and me and thank us for being a big help while she's been under a lot of strain. She'll even smile at Dad like everything's okay between them. Trouble is, she can't quite pull off the family-togetherness thing anymore. It's fake — something else she's programmed, practiced, and scheduled. And surer than hell, she'll be fidgeting and looking at her watch before the movie's half over."

He looked down and cleared his throat. "It's not that I don't love her. It's just that I can't figure out why she let her success chew up their marriage and just about everything else in our lives."

"Well, couldn't they see a marriage counselor, or something? I mean — "

He shook his head. "No, they're way beyond that. They used to go to counseling, and when they weren't doing that, they'd fight. Now they don't do either. They're just staying out of each other's way until it's the right time to make splitting up official."

"But — "

"Look, their marriage is shot, man. You know what *the Mom* says? She says she's 'outgrown' Dad. Said it in a letter I stumbled on in her hard drive one day. It was to somebody named Ben, and from the sound of it, Ben's not just a friend. So I figure she's getting her share on the side. And I know damn well Dad is, because I came by his office one afternoon last spring after everyone else had knocked off for the day, and there was this bimbo from accounting in his office. They weren't going over the expense account."

It took me a minute to process that. "My God, did they see you?"

"Nah. They were too busy. Hell, the university band could have marched through and they wouldn't have noticed."

What could I say? Images of my uncle Jerry and some bimbo making it on . . . On what? The desk? The floor? And Randy standing at the door, his mouth open, and then slowly backing out into the shadows of the darkened corridor. "Uh, did you say anything later?"

"I thought about it. But then I figured, what the hell? My parents' marriage is finished. They're both screwing around. Why should I get involved? I'll just make the best of things until they decide to tell us they're getting divorced. The Little D, I call it. Goes along with the Big D."

"I'm sorry."

He shrugged. "Yeah . . . Well, maybe it'd be better for them to knock off all the faking and get it done. Then we could all just get on with our lives."

"How's Marcia going to handle it?"

"Oh, she'll do okay. She always does. She's twelve going on about thirty. Nothing fazes her. But do you know what really pisses me off? It's not Marcia they're worried about; it's me. Poor Randy with his diabetes. For the last five years, I've been trying to prove that I'm no wimp, but they don't get it. You ought to see this list of rules *the Mom* wrote for me. What I can't eat, where I can't go, what sports I can't play . . . just pages and pages of rules. She even had her *secretary* reduce it on the copier and staple it into a little booklet for me to carry."

"You got it along?"

"Hell, no. I left it on the hall table just to piss her off."

"And your dad agrees with all this stuff?"

"Oh, he at least tries to keep her off my back some of the time. But he's pretty paranoid, too, always asking me if I'm testing enough, eating right, switching around the location of the shots . . . all the stuff I've been doing for years."

"But if they're so paranoid all the time, why'd they send you on this trip?"

He didn't say anything for a minute, and when he

answered, his voice was husky. "It took me a long time to figure that out. This is the big test. If I do okay, they can say: 'Okay, the wimp's old enough to make it on his own. So pass the divorce papers. Okay, who gets the china? Who gets the silverware? Who gets which kid when?' " He turned, his eyes glistening with tears. "Ain't that the pits, man? When I finally prove I'm no wimp, that's when they split up. I can't win." He turned away quickly.

We sat in silence for a long time. The breeze had pushed us into the shadow of the big island, the hull of the canoe rippling the reflection of the cedars and pines clinging to the granite shore. Half a dozen ducks flew over, and I watched them until they disappeared into the blue distance to the north, where water met land and land sky along the shimmering line of the horizon. And even after listening to Randy, even after hearing the dirty secrets of adultery in after-hours offices and of parents who no longer cared enough to play it straight with their kids, I still felt good, still felt that all that had happened very far away and, like my own small troubles, could never really matter here.

I reached down and ran my hand through the clear water, feeling the cold running up my fingers to my wrist. Here nothing mattered except rain and wind, water and sky, as the seasons turned, one after another, as they always had. We were about as significant as water bugs. Maybe less so. And somehow, that didn't scare me anymore.

I cleared my throat. "Randy," I said, "you know, we can't change anything going on back there. Not from here. So maybe we ought to just forget about it and try to enjoy the rest of the day. We might even catch a fish or two."

He snorted. "Who gives a damn about catching —"

"Hey, it's fish or a freeze-dried supper."

He looked down at his fishing pole. "You know, when you put it that way, I do give a damn."

"Besides, you promised to catch a big one."

He looked at me, managing a smile that broadened into a grin. "Yeah, I did, didn't I? Okay. Let's do it. Try to catch some fish and try to have a good time."

"Sounds good to me, partner. Put the ash to it, and we'll give it a whirl over by shore."

We landed a couple of fish but no keepers along the eastern shore of the big island. We ate lunch on a strip of beach below a broken cliff of granite, and then on a whim, climbed to the top to see if we could get a better view of the northern end of the lake. The climb looked easier than it was, and we were both winded by the time we scrambled onto the cliff top. We caught our breath and then angled upward through stunted pine and spruce, whose roots twisted across the thin soil in search of a hold on the rock. The higher we got, the more bent and misshapen the trees became until they gave way entirely and we came out on a windswept table of granite with the lakes and the land outspread in a great circle around us.

"Hey," Randy said. "Will you take a look at that view?"

I didn't say anything, because there was no point in

saying anything. So I just stood, letting the colors and the space have me.

After a few minutes, Randy said, "What do you suppose caused that?"

"Caused what?"

"That funny looking little island over there." He pointed.

A small island, shaped almost like a hat with the crown torn away and a bite out of the rim, lay a few hundred yards offshore. "I don't know," I said. "You're the geologist."

"I wish. That is really weird how it's almost hollowed out like a doughnut."

"Maybe your big fish lives there."

"Could be. Come on, let's go check it out."

"You're getting hyper just like your dad. Let's sit here and enjoy the view for a few minutes."

He let me have about three minutes before he was up and antsy to get going. We made our way back through the trees and then carefully down the cliff to the canoe. We paddled around the northern end of the big island, catching sight of the smaller island as soon as we cleared the point below the overlook.

From lake level, the island looked no stranger than any other. Only if you'd seen it from above or happened by the narrow break in the rim would you know that it was hollowed out, the sides of the crown embracing a quiet bay untouched by waves or wind. At the entrance, the water shallowed and we scraped several times getting through. But once we'd slid into the shadow beneath the high walls of the bay, the water went straight down into a bowl so deep and so still it felt somehow wrong to dip a paddle.

"Wow," Randy said, "it must be a hundred feet — Hey, look at the fish!"

I looked and saw first one, then three, then half a dozen thick brown forms swimming slowly deep, deep down. "Must be some kind of lake trout," I said.

"Think we can catch one?" Randy picked up his pole and started lowering his lure over the side.

"Not that way. You'll have to put on big sinkers to get a bait down there."

"Shall we do it?"

I studied the fish. "I doubt if we could get one up even if we hooked it. Our line is pretty light and those things are big, Randy. Real big."

"Well, we could at least try."

I leaned back, staring up into the dark green shadows in the cliffs around us. And for some reason, I shivered. This was not a place people came often, not a place to disturb lightly. "No, it's not worth it, Randy. Even if you hook one of those beasts, it's not going to let you bring it up. No way. Let's just leave 'em be."

He set down his pole unwillingly. "Well, okay, if it's not worth the effort . . ."

"It's not."

He looked around. "So are we going to sit here, or are we going to find something we can catch?"

"Just relax and listen for a minute."

He listened for about ten seconds. "What am I supposed to be listening to?"

"Nothing."

He turned to look at me. "That's pretty dumb."

"Yeah. Nothing's pretty dumb all right. Never says a word."

"Huh?"

"Never mind," I said. I took a last look around, memorizing what I'd never paint but wanted to remember.

We fished the water between the two islands without success and then decided to try our luck along the eastern shore of the lake. I was hoping that we'd finished with the subject of families for the day, but he started in on it again when we were maybe halfway across the open water. "How about your folks?" he asked. "They get along okay?"

"No big problems that I know of."

"Your mom's got a new job, huh?"

"Yeah, she's the librarian at the twins' school. That's a lot better for me, because I don't have to baby-sit three days a week like when she was working in the Anoka County library. The twins go down to the library and look at books until she knocks off for the day."

"They pretty good kids?"

"If you like high volume and lots of fights. They've been doing a 'difficult-age' number on Mom and Dad for about the last two years."

"Whoa. I thought teenagers were supposed to have a lock on the 'difficult-age' number. Those kids are on our turf."

"Hey, they can have all the turf and all the attention they want. Less time for Mom and Dad to get on my case."

97

"About Sonia?"

"Well, the grades more. Sonia's pretty recent, but I've been just getting by in school for a long time. My third-quarter report was really bad, and Dad grounded me all spring except for Saturdays. That's about the same time he started talking about this trip a lot."

"So this trip really is supposed to straighten your ass out. Big coming-of-age experience, huh?"

"That's the main idea, I guess, but let's not forget family tradition."

"Oh, yeah. Dear old Grandpa breaking a path through the wilderness when it really was wilderness. As my sister would say, 'Big, fat, hairy deal.'"

We'd reached the eastern side of the lake and paddled south as the sun began to fall and our silhouette started to stretch out toward the shore. We were getting less choosy about what to keep, and after an hour, we had two small walleyes and a couple of bluegills trailing behind on the stringer. "We'd better turn around pretty soon," I said. "It'll take us at least an hour to get home."

"Let's try that little opening first. I'd like to catch one decent fish."

"I'd settle for an indecent fish. I don't care about its morals."

"Ha, ha. Stick with the Boy Scout stories; you're better at them."

I swung the bow into the inlet, and then backwatered. "Too shallow here, we're going to get hung up."

"Just hold it long enough for me to make a couple of casts. I've got a feeling about this place."

I snorted. "You and your — "

Randy's lure hit the water and disappeared like he'd snagged a bowling ball. A second later, a fish half as long as the canoe exploded from the water, slashing back and forth with an ugly snout lined with sharp teeth. "Holy shit!" I yelled. "Don't bring that thing in here."

He didn't listen. Instead, he heaved back on the line, and reeled in like crazy. The fish jumped again, trying to throw the bait, but Randy had it hooked hard. He reeled faster. "Net it," he yelled, as the fish swirled up alongside the canoe.

"I don't want to net it!"

"Net it, you wimp!"

I grabbed the net out of the bottom of the canoe and tried to get it under the fish. There was more fish than net, and when I slung the net up, it flopped out, landing smack in the middle of the canoe, where it leaped and flopped and made at least one attempt to bite my leg off. I slammed a foot down on its neck and then got the other on its tail. It tried to toss me out of the canoe, but I bore down and it stopped flopping, its ugly mouth sucking as it tried to breathe air. Randy was cheering. "Dinner! Way to go, partner."

"Right. Now what the hell am I supposed to do? It's going to attack if I let it up."

Randy studied the fish. "Do you suppose you could put it on the stringer?"

"Not on your life. You see those teeth?"

"Yeah, they do look kind of scary, don't they?"

"*Scary*? It nearly took my foot off."

"You're exaggerating. What kind of fish is it, anyway?"

99

"Northern pike, I think. Now, come on. What're we gonna do with it?"

"Maybe if you hold it there for a minute, it'll die."

"It's going to live for hours. Or until we gut it."

"Well, there you go then. Here, I'll paddle us over to shore."

Sitting backward, he managed to get us through the shallows. He climbed out, pulled the canoe broadside to the shore, and squatted to study his trophy. "Would you hurry up?" I snapped.

"Relax. I just want to have a good look at it. It ain't gonna hurt you."

"Easy for you to say. The knife is in the tackle box."

He got it out. "Okay," he said. "Where's its heart?"

"How would I know where its heart is? Just cut its head off. And watch my foot while you're doing it."

Randy slit the northern's throat and then sawed away as the fish writhed under my feet. Finally, he severed its head, and I kicked it under the bow seat where it gave a few more disgruntled snaps before giving up the fight. I lifted my other foot gingerly, not sure I trusted the fish even without its head.

"How much do you think it weighs?" Randy asked.

"How would I know? You're the expert fisherman these days."

"I guess we might as well let the others go. This one's going to be more than we can eat."

When I'd let the small fish go, Randy climbed back in and we started the paddle home. He was still glowing, anxious to talk about the glory of his catch. "Yeah, yeah," I said. "You're a stud fisherman, Charlie. But I did the dangerous stuff."

"What do you mean? I was the one who cut its head off."

"Yeah, but I was the one who almost lost some toes."

"Hey, small sacrifice for a fish dinner. Come on, partner. Let's put the old ash to 'er."

It was the best fish I'd ever eaten. When we'd gorged ourselves like a pair of pythons, we tossed a couple of logs on the fire and leaned back. Randy gave a satisfied grunt. "God, that was good. I don't know if I'm ever going to be able to eat that freeze-dried crap again." He started fussing with his blood tester.

"Need some light?" I asked.

"Thanks. That'd help."

I held the flashlight while he did the test and gave himself a shot in the thigh. "Your legs are looking better all the time," I said.

"Thanks, but you're still not my type." He repacked his kit and stuck it in the food pack. "Shall we hang this while we've got the energy?"

"Sure," I said.

We were getting better at the routine and got the pack good and high, well out of reach of anything except maybe an elephant or a giraffe. "There," I said. "Let's make some cocoa."

"Great idea. Too bad the cocoa's in the pack."

"No, it isn't. I took it out."

"Hey, good thinking, partner. Toss it here; I'll make it."

"Be my guest." I settled back against my boulder and looked out across the lake.

"You know," he said, "when I make the big-time

101

lawyer bucks, I think maybe I'll buy a fishing boat. One of those big ones you can take out onto Lake Michigan or Lake Superior."

"You want to be a lawyer, or is that your mom's idea?"

He shrugged. "More hers than mine, I guess. At least I'd make a lot of money."

"What would you rather be?"

He hesitated. "Well, I really am interested in geology. What I told you about the Canadian Shield was more than I learned in school. I've read some books."

"What's wrong with geology if that's what you want to do?"

"Mom says I'd end up teaching for peanuts in some Podunk college or going to work for a big oil company where there's not a lot of job security these days. She says the law's better."

"And you always listen to her?"

"Well, she usually knows what she's talking about. At least when it comes to making money. But . . . Well, I'm keeping the options open. How about you? What do you want to do?"

"I have no idea."

"Oh, come on. Everybody does."

I shrugged. "I used to want to be — don't laugh, now — an artist."

"What's funny about that?"

"Nothing, other than I was no damned good at art."

"Who said?"

"My art teacher, for one. She said that I used too much paint, which was probably true, and that I wasn't interested in listening to directions, which was only partly true."

"How's that?"

"Well, I wanted to learn about perspective and painting from models and all that stuff. But I'd kind of get involved in something else about the picture and it'd never turn out like the other kids'. I got laughed at a lot."

"So you quit trying."

"No, I had all sorts of art stuff at home, and I painted a lot. Trouble is, my dad's an engineer and knows all that stuff about perspective and drawing things just right. So whenever I'd show him a picture, he'd want to start making it just as accurate as a blueprint. But it was messing with the colors that interested me. And then good old Bob got after me. And he, of course, knows how to draft and draw just as well as Dad does. And he was going to get me to do it right no matter what and to hell with all this artsy color stuff. That's when I quit."

"How long ago was that?"

"On my thirteenth birthday. That day I decided to grow up, so I packed up all my oils and watercolors and stuck 'em in the attic."

"Too bad."

"Not really. I was no damned good at it, and I don't miss it. I still like to imagine a picture sometimes, but that's as far as I need to take it."

"Yeah, but what are you going to do with your life?"

"I'll get by. I don't need to be Bob or my dad. Something will come along." He looked unhappy, as if he —

like just about everybody else in my life — figured I ought to have some goal beyond sliding by. I interrupted him before he could say anything. "If you're still planning on making cocoa, you'd better take that water off before it boils away."

"Oh, yeah." He pulled the pot off the fire, dumped in the cocoa, and gave it a few stirs. The conversation wandered on to other subjects as we drank the cocoa and watched the fire. After a while, he started to doze and then shook himself. "I'm falling asleep. I'm going to wash up, brush my teeth, and go to bed."

"I'll be along," I said.

After he'd gone off to the tent, I sat on the ledge to watch the moon rise It came up full and orange, its light sliding across the lake toward the yellow reflection of our fire dancing at the water's edge. A loon chortled, bragging to its mate about something it had speared deep in the watery darkness beneath the moonlight. Not bad, I thought. Not bad at all. Maybe Dad and Uncle Jerry and their dad before them had been right about finding something up here. What exactly, I couldn't say. Maybe it didn't have a name. But that evening, as I listened to the loons calling, I think I touched it.

CHAPTER SIX

I came awake after the moon had set and the night couldn't get any darker, and lay for a time listening to the wind rustling high in the branches of the trees. I thought I heard a splash on the far side of our island or perhaps farther away still, out on the black waters of Ax Handle. But when I listened for it again, I heard only the sleepy rustling of the wind and the soft rippling of water against the shore. Probably a fish jumping or a loon landing, I told myself, and burrowed deeper into my sleeping bag.

Randy shook me awake in the gray first light. "There's something out there," he hissed.

"What?"

"Whisper, damn it. I don't know what it is, but I heard it moving in the brush."

I shook my head, trying to clear the fog. "Maybe a squirrel — "

"It wasn't any squirrel. It was big. Real big."

"Oh, come on. There isn't anything really big around here except — " And then I heard it, too, and my throat seized up before I could finish the sentence.

"What is it?" Randy whined, his voice on the edge of panic.

Visions of bearded homicidal maniacs, gigantic grizzlies, and a northern Minnesota version of the Loch Ness monster competed for top billing in my imagination. Finally, I managed, "I don't know. I guess it's probably a bear. Why don't you look?"

"Why don't *you?*"

"Okay, okay," I said. As quietly as I could, I wrestled the sleeping bag down to my waist and peeked out the window.

Randy pushed in beside me, and together we peered into the shadowy brush. We couldn't see anything. "What should we do?" he whispered.

"I don't know. Maybe we should just stay real quiet."

"What happens if it comes over here? I don't want to be eaten in the tent."

"Bears don't eat people. Not unless they're starving or something."

"Well, who says it's not starving?"

"It can't be starving, it's summertime."

"Well, I'm getting out, anyway." He reached for the tent flap, but just then the bear — or whatever it was — decided to wander in our direction. We huddled against the far wall of the tent as gigantic paws — or boots, claws, or flippers — crunched toward us across the pine needles. Then it stopped, seemed to hesitate, snorted a couple of times, and moved off toward the shore. Randy lunged for the tent flap.

I was right behind him, and we stood shivering together in the gray light beside the huge boulder shadowing our tent. We still couldn't see it, and for a second

I had the wild hope that maybe it really was something small enough to hide in the brush — maybe a very noisy porcupine or a big raccoon or just possibly a heavy-footed squirrel. Then a tree near the fire pit started shaking. "What the hell?" I said. We took a couple of steps and spotted it — black and big and very much a bear — standing on its hind legs, slowly rocking the tree.

"What's he doing?" Randy asked.

"Trying to knock down our food pack, I think."

"Hey, bear! Get away from there," Randy yelled, making me jump about a yard in the air.

The bear ignored him. "For God's sake, shut up," I hissed.

"But — "

"Just take it easy, damn it. He's pissed that he can't reach that high or climb a tree that small. He'll give up in a minute."

But the bear kept pushing and within a lot less than a minute, we heard some ominous creaking. "Oh, shit," Randy said, "the pole's starting to give." He reached into the tent, grabbed his jacket, and started waving it at the bear. "Hey, get away from there, bear! Go on, get out of here." The bear didn't even glance our way, and a second later, there was a loud crack, the sound of splintering, and the food pack thudded to the ground. I swear the bear gave a grunt of satisfaction before dropping his forefeet to the ground and rolling the pack over with a huge paw. Randy's diabetes kit fell out and the bear nosed it. And Randy charged the bear.

I couldn't believe it. I ran after him, shouting for

him to stop. Instead, he stooped, snatched up a rock, and fired it at the bear. "Are you crazy?" I yelled, but he ignored me and reached for another rock. I grabbed him. "Leave that damned thing alone. It's big enough to eat us both."

He tried to twist away, but I held on. "You idiot," he snarled. "Didn't you pay attention to anything I told you? I've got to have food or I'm in real deep shit."

For a second, I'd forgotten. "Oh, shit," I said, let go of him, and reached for a rock.

The bear didn't pay any attention to us, not even flinching as we bounced half a dozen rocks off his body. He sat down on his backside with the rocks and curses whizzing around him, pulled the pack between his legs, and calmly began sorting through our food. It was just like some Disney nature show where the bears act more human than the humans. But this was real, and it got a lot more real when Randy hit him square on the side of the head with a rock the size of a grapefruit. That got his attention. He shook his head, looked at us, and then lunged to his feet with a very unpleasant snort and a sound like he was snapping his teeth through a leg bone. We got the hint and moved. Fast. I fell over a tree root, stubbing at least six toes, but with images of the bear about to sink his teeth in my ass, I didn't waste any time rolling around on the ground in pain. Ahead of me, Randy scrambled up the side of the big boulder beside our tent. I was a second behind him, clawing my way to the top with my fingers and toes gripping the stone like an ape's. Back by the pack, the bear gave a well-I-guess-I-showed-them grunt and sat down to finish his breakfast.

We sat atop the boulder as the day got lighter with the rising sun and the bear got fatter on our food. Peanut-butter sandwich cookies topped his list, followed by my Snickers bars, Randy's granola bars, the trail mix, and so on down the menu, which didn't seem to contain anything too unappetizing to eat. He even ate the freeze-dried crap, tearing open the packets, sniffing the contents, and then stuffing his mouth full. "We've got another package of that spaghetti, don't we?" I asked. "Maybe that'll poison him." Randy didn't reply, and I didn't make any more attempts at joking.

Finally, the bear was done. He stood, shook himself, nosed through the paper and foil a final time, and moseyed our way. Below the boulder, he stared up at us and snapped his jaws a couple of times, but there seemed little real interest in his tiny eyes. We retreated to the far side of the boulder and watched as he poked his head into our tent, snuffled around the tent pack lying next to a tree, and then sauntered back toward the shore. He sat down and stared out over the lake, probably considering what other mayhem he could commit before noon. "I think he's going to take a nap," I said.

"Oh, great," Randy muttered.

"Well, we could try to cut his throat while he's sleeping. Then we'd at least have bear meat to eat."

"Will you shut up? You're not making things any better."

I glanced at him. He looked like he was about to cry. "Sorry," I said. "Just trying to fill the silence."

The bear roused himself and, without so much as a glance toward us, lumbered down to the water, waded in, and with a thrust of his powerful hind legs, pushed off into the lake. Within five minutes, he was only a speck far out on the water, swimming easily toward the eastern shore.

We climbed down and went to look at the damage. Randy picked up his diabetes kit. "Look," he said, pointing to the imprint of claws, "the damned thing stepped right on it." He unzipped it and poked at the contents. "It's okay. Nothing's — Oh, shit."

"What?"

"The Glucotron's cracked." He held it up to show me an inch-long crack in the plastic back. He shook it by his ear. "Nothing sounds broken." He punched a couple of buttons. "Yeah, I think it's okay."

We gathered up the remains of our food. The bear had rejected the dehydrated potatoes and onions and he'd missed a couple of granola bars deep in a side pocket, but all the rest of our food was slopping happily around in his stomach. Or so I thought until we gathered up the paper and foil and found a single unopened package of freeze-dried food. Spaghetti. I tossed it to Randy. "The SOB was too smart to eat it."

Randy grunted. "It figures. There are some packets of cocoa over here."

"How many?"

"Three."

"We had a lot more."

"Well, he ate the rest. You got anything in your pockets?"

I searched. "A couple of sticks of gum." I tossed them on the small pile. He added a small tin. "What's that?" I asked.

"Butterscotch drops. Emergency sugar."

We sat staring at the little we had left. Finally, I asked, "How long do you think we can make this last?"

He sighed. "I don't know. How fast can we get back to the resort?"

I thought. "That depends on what route we take. Two days, maybe."

"It didn't take us quite two days to get here."

"Yeah, but the resort is all the way on the other end of Cant Hook, and that's at least half a day's paddle. It might be faster to go west and then south. Let me get the map, and we'll have a look."

He nodded and got out his Glucotron. "I've got to test this thing. Find out for sure if it still works."

I went to find the map in the tent pack while he messed with the Glucotron. When I got back, he was frowning at it. "What's the matter?" I asked.

He shook it and then studied the reading again. "It's a funny number, that's all. Higher than it should be by quite a bit."

"How do you feel?"

"Fine. But that's not a very good way to tell. Sometimes you can be way out of balance and feeling real good at the same time. Then the Big D sneaks up behind you and, *wham*, you're suddenly feeling like warmed-over crap. Here, let me borrow one of your fingers."

"Say what?"

"Come on. If you test normal, the tester will be okay."

"It's called a Glucotron, you dumb shit."

"Yeah, right. Come on, hold out a finger."

111

I did, and he zapped me with the needle gizmo. While he waited for the reading, I unfolded the map and started looking for a way out of this mess. He grunted. "Well, you're pretty much normal, so I guess it's working okay." He dug into his kit for a bottle of insulin. "So you figured out how to get us home?"

"I'm working on it." I pointed to the route Dad had penciled across Ax Handle. "It's a little shorter to go west like we'd planned. When we saw the bear the day before yesterday, we were just a couple of miles north of the portage to Talking Bird. That's a pretty big lake, but it won't take us too long to work along the south shore to this river running south into the next lake. Which is . . ." I unfolded another square of the map. "Hog Snout Lake."

"Hog Snout? God, where do they come up with these names?"

"Beats me. Anyway, the portage runs alongside the river and then cuts off to hit this bay. From what I can tell, that'll be the only really long portage the whole way back."

"What do those Roman numerals next to the river mean?"

"They're something to do with the rapids. Some kind of rating system. Dad explained it, but I didn't pay much attention since he said to portage all the rapids."

"Yeah, but I think things have changed some."

I hesitated. I wasn't any fan of portages, but I'd seen enough outdoor adventure movies to have a healthy fear of rapids. "Well, we'll have to look at them when we get there. Anyway, things get easier once we cross

Hog Snout. There's no portage trail and no rapids marked on the river between Hog Snout and Black Dan, so it must be safe to paddle that one. Then there's only a short portage to Big Carry and then the Carry River to Cant Hook, unless . . ." I hesitated.

"What?"

"Well, I guess there must be another short portage on that river. See where they've got Roman numeral four and a dotted line along the left shore. My guess is that's a short portage around a rapids."

"That four is in red. Must be a real big rapids."

"Probably. Anyway, the river empties into Cant Hook a couple of miles from the resort. We might even be able to see it from the mouth of the river."

"So, how long to get there from here?"

I hesitated again, not wanting to give him any false hope. "Well, they gave us two days from Talking Bird, but that was taking it easy. I think if we start soon, we should be able to make it to the far side of Hog Snout tonight and maybe get the rest of the way by sometime late tomorrow afternoon." I looked at him. "What do you think?"

"That's not too bad. We should have enough food for that."

"I don't have to eat. Hell, I was planning on losing a few pounds on this trip, anyway."

He looked at me and, for the first time that day, he grinned. "Well, partner, I can't say it'd hurt. It might be nice for you to see your richard without leaning over."

"Nice guy. I offer you my food and you give me a shot."

He laughed. "Sorry. Just couldn't pass it up. Okay, let's get going."

While we were packing the gear, I said, "We could throw a bait in the water every now and then. We had pretty good luck the last couple of days."

"Fishing takes time, and . . ." He hesitated. "Well, I'm kind of nervous about the Glucotron. Yeah, you tested normal, but who's to say that was accurate? Your blood sugar goes up and down, too, and you could have been twenty points low without any trouble at all. And that would mean I was even higher than it said. Like way high."

"I'm not sure I follow all this."

"Well, maybe I'm being paranoid, but I'd just rather not depend on this Glucotron any longer than I have to. It's just too chancy. So I think we'd better forget about the fishing and try to get back just as soon as we can." He hesitated. "I'm sorry, man. I was really enjoying all this." He gestured toward the lake.

I cleared my throat, surprised at the sudden lump that made it hard to talk. "Yeah, so was I. But, we don't have to have a bad time on the way back. If we keep moving, we shouldn't have to worry."

"Yeah, maybe we'll get lucky. Find a friendly Indian village or something. Maybe even a couple of real friendly Indian girls."

"Or at least we might run into another canoeing party," I said. "I've got five or ten bucks, and maybe they'll sell us some food. Then we could take it easy."

"You have your fantasy, I'll have mine. Well, let's do it." He hefted the tent pack, and I followed with what was now a very light food pack.

*　　*　　*

A couple of hundred yards from shore, we paused to look back at our island, sitting deserted and mournful against a gray sky. "It was all right," Randy said. "I was even planning to dive off the ledge this morning."

"It'd be colder today."

Randy gazed at the sky. "Yeah, it looks like the bear took our nice weather, too. But I would have done it just to prove that my ass is every bit as hairy as yours."

"I never doubted it," I said. Or if I had, I'd long since thought differently.

We put the ash to it, paddling west against a stiff wind. We ducked through the islands, taking advantage of what shelter we could, and then crossed the long stretch of open water toward the portage to Talking Bird. We didn't talk much, couldn't have if we'd wanted to, as the clouds dropped low and the wind began to eddy.

As long as we'd had the packing and the planning to do, I'd been able to stop myself from thinking too much about facing Dad. I knew he'd blame me for this mess, even though we'd done exactly as we'd been told. Or maybe we hadn't. Maybe somewhere along the line, Dad or Uncle Jerry had warned us about trees too small to stop a smart bear. I couldn't remember, but it didn't make any difference. I'd get the blame. And, damn it, that wasn't fair. Because I'd tried, really tried for once, to do things just as well as my brother . . . My eyes started to sting, and I bit my lip. Come on, damn it. Stop acting like a crybaby. You've got to move this boat. You can worry about the other stuff later, but right now, you've got to keep paddling. I leaned into it, feeling Randy adjust as I picked up the pace. He didn't say anything, and I guessed that his thoughts were as dismal as mine.

We had the portage in sight when a rain squall burst from an eddy of low dark clouds to the southwest. Damn, this was going to be hard enough dry; wet it'd be agony. "We'd better move it," I shouted. "If we can get on shore, we can set up the tent until this blows over."

Randy dug in, and we pushed hard for the portage. We made it just as the first big drops hit the water around us. Randy jumped out, grabbed the bow and pulled us up on the muddy shore. I shoved my paddle out of the way under my seat, threw him the food pack, and scrambled out with the tent pack.

"Where?" he yelled.

"Let's try over there." I pointed to a little break in the trees a few dozen yards away.

The rain was coming harder, and we could hear the wind building in the trees as we unrolled the tent, jammed the pegs in as far as we could, and got the poles upright. "Should we turn over the canoe?" he yelled.

A gust of rain sluiced over the lake. "Forget it. We'll dump it out afterward. Get in. I'm right behind you." I chucked the packs and life preservers in after him and dove inside. The squall hit with a roar just as I zipped the flap shut.

We unrolled the sleeping bags and lay waiting for the rain to let up. Randy shook his watch. "Damn, I thought I had it working again. What time do you have?"

I stretched and looked at my watch. "Just about noon." I started to add "I'm hungry," but caught myself.

Randy dug out his Glucotron and ran the test. "Shit. I'm still high. Jeez, I can't understand that. This damned thing must be broken."

I sat up to peek out the window. "It's still coming down like crazy. I can't even see the islands."

"I think I'm going to eat one of those granola bars. My blood sugar just can't be that high. Not after all the work."

"Go ahead."

He dug one out of the pack and hesitated. "We've only got two, and I really ought to save the other one for emergencies."

"Don't worry about it. I'm okay."

He unwrapped the bar and took a bite. "Well, you can have your full share of the spaghetti tonight."

"Don't do me any favors." I looked out the window again. And then it hit me. I yelled, "Shit," and nearly knocked the tent down getting through the flap. The canoe was gone. I peered through the driving rain, finally picking it out a good two hundred yards off-shore, drifting merrily away on a steady southwest wind.

Randy stood beside me, water running off the bill of his cap and the half-eaten granola bar forgotten in his hand. "Oh, shit," he said. "Now what do we do?"

I concluded a minute of creative swearing by kicking a rock for emphasis, which was a particularly dumbshit thing to do since I got an instant reminder of stubbing my toes that morning while trying to keep the bear from biting me in the ass. I limped over to the tent and started pulling off my clothes. "Get on your poncho," I snapped. "Then go up the shore. I'll swim out and try to pull it in. Or paddle it in, if I can figure out how to get in without capsizing it."

"I'll go," he said. "It's my fault; I should have pulled it up farther."

"Damn it, it's just as much my fault as yours! Just get your poncho — "

"Hey, don't order me around, man!" He started pulling off his shirt. "I swim just as well as you do. Probably better."

I stopped, one pant leg off and the rain splattering on my bare back. I tried to speak calmly. "Look, we both know you can't spare the energy. Not if we're going to make it on the food we've got. Now are we going to fight about this until the damned canoe is out of sight, or am I going to go get it?"

He hesitated, and then pulled his shirt back on. "Okay," he said. "You're right. But be careful, huh?"

"I'll try. Just have my clothes waiting when I get back." I limped to the shore, waded out as far as I could, and dove in.

Tough. God, I'd never done anything so tough in my life. No matter how hard I swam, I gained only slowly on the canoe as the wind pushed it out into the wide water to the northeast. I tried to keep my mind off the cold by counting my strokes, looking up every twenty to see if the canoe had grown any larger. When my arms got heavy, I thought of floating on my back, but I was afraid that my muscles would cramp if I rested. So I concentrated on my anger to keep me going. Of all the stupid stunts . . . God, we were almost too dumb to live.

After what seemed like forever, the squall blew over, the wind dropped, and the canoe stopped drifting. Damn good thing, too, because I didn't have much left in the tank. A half-dozen gulls swept low over me, curious and then amused, squawking to each other before flying on toward the lightening sky to the west. I could just make out the license numbers on the bow of the canoe, and I concentrated on them until I could read each number. Then I recited them over and over, until, with a final stroke, I reached the canoe. I got a hand over the stern and hung there for a couple of minutes, getting my breath. From the shore, I heard Randy shouting. I waved a hand to tell him that I was all right and started considering the next problem. I could try to pull the canoe by the bow rope — the rope any other damned fool would have tied to a tree before worrying about the tent — or I could try to get in over the stern and paddle to shore.

I got my hands on either side of the stern, kicked hard, and tried to muscle up so I could flop in over the rear seat. The canoe suddenly got very tippy, and I fell back into the water. Okay, jerk, be careful. You are really going to be screwed if you tip this damned thing over. I tried again and managed to get my elbows locked and the point of the stern against my stomach. Now if I could just work my hands forward a little . . . I lost my grip and fell, the point of the stern raking my belly as the canoe bucked away. I felt for blood, felt only a long scratch, and tried again. This time I didn't

119

even get my elbows locked before I lost my grip on the slippery aluminum and nearly capsized the canoe. Enough, damn it. Swim for it while you've still got the strength.

I swam to the bow and found the rope. I tried paddling on my back with the rope between my teeth, but that didn't work worth a damn. So I looped it around my chest, and started doing a slow, painful crawl toward shore. So help me, if I got through this trip alive, I'd never go near more water than filled a bathtub. Not even for Sonia. If she just *had* to go to the water park, she could go by herself. Or with somebody else. I didn't care anymore.

Ahead I could make out Randy squatting on the shore. He was doing something in front of him, but I couldn't make out what until I caught sight of a tiny flicker of orange. He was trying to build a fire, and — incredibly — he seemed to be getting somewhere. The thought of warmth gave me a last burst of adrenaline and, after what seemed another eternity, I finally touched bottom. My feet were so numb that I slipped and fell twice before I managed to get my legs under me. Randy took a step into the shallows and put out a hand. "I'm okay," I panted. "Keep your feet dry." I made the last couple of yards to him and he grabbed the bow and pulled it well up onto the beach. Shivering uncontrollably, I collapsed next to the loveliest thing I'd ever seen in life: the fire.

"God, how'd you get it going?" I chattered.

"I had a good teacher." He pulled a towel from under a poncho and started rubbing me down. "I've got your clothes and a dry pair of underwear," he said. I reached down and tried to get my underwear off, but my fingers weren't working. "Here," he said. He grabbed the elastic, pulled them down over my ankles, and dropped the towel in my lap. "You can dry your own richard, man. I ain't that much your pal."

He threw another armload of branches on the fire and then helped me into my clothes. As the fire blazed up, I moved back a little and at last started getting some feeling in my hands and feet. "You gonna be okay?" Randy asked.

"Yeah, I think so."

He went to the far side of the fire and brought back a cup of cocoa. "I didn't want to give you this before; you were shaking too hard. Don't worry, I boiled the water."

I took a swallow, the hot going all the way down to my groin. "God, that's great," I said. I let myself drink half the cup and then held it out to him. "You finish."

"It's okay; we've got enough."

"Where's yours, then?" He shrugged. "We don't have enough. You finish. By then I'll be ready." He hesitated, and then took the cup.

He made me sit by the fire until it burned down, and then we towed the canoe down the shore to the portage. When we got to the tent, he said, "Do you want to go on? We could camp here."

"We'd lose a lot of time and maybe have to spend another night out. I don't know if that'd be smart." He didn't say anything. "Well, what do you think?"

He sighed. "Yeah, I guess that might be cutting it a little close."

"Let's get over the portage, then. The wind's down and maybe we'll make better time on Talking Bird."

"Okay," he said. "If you're sure you're up for it."

"Yeah, I'm up for it."

I said so then, but the long swim had taken more out of me than I realized. I had to call a halt when we were halfway across the portage and then again when we had the lake in sight. By the time we finally swung the canoe off our shoulders and dropped the packs, I felt light-headed. "We'd better camp," Randy said. "You look like crap." I nodded, too tired to argue.

Randy built the fire, and I got the tent up, my hands refusing to do what I told them to unless I concentrated all my attention on every movement. When the fire was going strong, Randy put on water to boil and spread the remaining food out in front of him. "I guess it didn't grow any," I said.

"Nope. This is all we've got. Still think we can get all the way back tomorrow?"

I unfolded the map and tried to focus on it. "Maybe, but I wouldn't bet on it. We'll have to start early and push like a son of a bitch until dark."

"Well, that's what we're going to have to do, then."

I felt myself starting to nod off as he boiled the water for the spaghetti. I levered myself to my feet, using his shoulder to push myself up. "Where you going?" he said.

"To bed. I'm not hungry."

"Come on. I don't want to eat all this crap by myself."

"Then save it for tomorrow. All I want to do is sleep."

I was too tired and too cold to bother taking off my

clothes. I pulled off my boots, crawled into my damp sleeping bag, and was asleep before I could even bother to feel sorry for myself. What seemed a long time later, I was vaguely aware of Randy getting his bed ready. Still later, I heard thunder and the first drops of a cold, steady rain.

CHAPTER
SEVEN

I dreamed of swimming far out under a night sky twisting with colors, and lying back in the gentle rocking of the water, feeling it deep beneath me all the way down farther than I could imagine, and wondering if the fish rose to the surface on the nights when the aurora burned in the sky to get a glimpse of color before going deep again where things hadn't changed except for the passing of the seasons and the generations in ten thousand years. And when the colors faded, I went down into sleep so deep that I had no sight at all but only the sense of huge nameless things swimming about me as we moved together, slowly and almost without effort, through the darkness.

I came awake, smelled wood smoke, and heard Randy banging pots and pans. I started to roll over, but the muscles in my body protested in a chorus of yelps, whines, and howls. God, what had I done to myself? I lay still for a minute, listening to the drizzle on the tent roof, and then tried again. It took me five minutes to get out of my sleeping bag, change my socks, and pull on my boots. Finally, I managed to crawl out of the tent and stand. "I'm alive," I said. "Barely."

"Yeah, I could tell by the groans. A little stiff, huh?"

"You can't imagine the half of it. For the first time I have some sympathy for the old guys."

"Nah, they're just faking it." He dumped the leftover spaghetti into a frying pan and started stirring it with a fork.

"How you doing?"

"Got another screwy reading on the Glucotron, but I feel fine, so I'm going to hold off on my first shot until noon or so. That way I figure the IJ and the food should balance out a little better." He tossed me a packet of cocoa mix. "The water's hot."

I pulled on my poncho and considered the cocoa mix. God, it'd taste good. "Sure there's enough?"

"If we can make it by late this afternoon, there shouldn't be any problem."

I dropped the cocoa back into the food pack. "Hot water will be fine," I said. "We might not make it until tomorrow morning."

He grimaced. "You know, it's pretty damned embarrassing to watch you go hungry on account of me."

"Don't bitch. It's going to be a hell of a lot more embarrassing if you pass out."

"I'm not going to pass out," he snapped.

"Good. Don't burn the spaghetti." I squatted by the fire and poured myself a cup of hot water. My stomach growled, and I sucked it in to shut it up.

Randy pulled the frying pan off the fire. "Grab a plate. There's still enough for two."

"Oh, no, you don't. You're not getting me to help you with that garbage. Eat hearty. I'm just fine."

"Turkey," he muttered, and started eating out of the frying pan. After the second bite, he made a face. "I wish I had a clothespin for my nose; this stuff smells even worse than it tastes." He reached in his pocket and tossed me the tin of butterscotch drops. "At least put one of these in your water. That'll give it some taste."

"Thanks," I said, and dropped one in. I studied the sky while he ate. It seemed lighter to the west, and I began to hold out some hope for the day. Oddly, I felt pretty good now that my body had limbered up.

I got out the map and had another look at our route. We had a long way to go, but if we pushed like hell, maybe we could get to the resort by nightfall. A big meal, a few games of pool, and then to bed on a real mattress between dry sheets. Almost enough to make one willing to suffer the grilling from Dad and Uncle Jerry.

A wind came up while we were loading the canoe, ruffling the surface of Talking Bird. To the west, the overcast began shredding, and the first patch of blue broke through the gray. "Looks like it might be a nice day, after all," I said.

Randy wasn't in the mood for silver linings and only glanced at the sky. "Just as long as we don't have to fight too much wind. What's the time, anyway?"

"A little after eight. You should have gotten me up earlier."

"I called you a couple of times, but you only groaned. You okay now?"

"I'm fine. I know I did something yesterday, but I'm okay."

"Yeah, that was quite a deal. The Mountain Man would be proud of you. Your dad and your brother, too."

"Dad maybe, not Bob the Nazi," I said. "But let's forget to mention it. We've got enough stupid things to explain."

"Well, you ought to tell your girl, anyway. Blame it on me and be the hero. Might as well get some credit."

Strange, but I hadn't thought of Sonia at all that morning. "Yeah, maybe I'll do that. If you don't mind."

He shrugged. "What do I care?" He pulled his poncho over his head and tossed it on the load in the canoe. "We'll be back home in a couple of days and this will be just a fond memory."

"It hasn't been all that bad. Except for the bear, of course. Next time, I'm going to bring one of those cable rigs we saw at the outfitter's and choose bigger trees."

"Next time? When's that going to be?"

"In about a thousand years. Just talking."

He shoved his paddle over to the other side of the bow and climbed in. "Well, I don't think my old man and *the Mom* are going to let me do anything like this again. Not when we show up with no food, a busted Glucotron, and some bad stories. Shove us off, we've got some miles to cover."

When we were well out in the lake, I said, "They're gonna be pissed, huh?"

"Oh, Dad won't blame me too much. He'll just . . .

Hell, I don't know. He's just going to be disappointed that the trip went to hell on us. And he'll start thinking that maybe *the Mom*'s been right all along: that I really can't do what other kids can. So I'll have to fight that battle all over again."

I angled the bow to cut into the wind a little better. "What's your mom going to do?"

"Well for starters, she'll ream out Dad so that he'll never have to worry about being constipated again. And then she'll make me sign about sixteen pages of new rules. Legal form, Dad and Marcia for witnesses."

"You're kidding."

"Uh-uh. She'll make it a contract. You can bet on it."

"Well, maybe your dad won't tell her."

"Dad? Shit, he can't keep anything secret. I bet she even knows about the bimbo from accounting. She'll grill him about the trip, and he'll sing. And after she's finished with him, she'll put me on the fire. And like as not, I'll sing, too. . . . Cripes, let's talk about something else. I'm going to have to deal with *the Mom* soon enough."

We paddled for half an hour without talking. The sun broke hot through the clouds and within minutes the woods to the south steamed with rising mist. A single day of bad weather behind us and now beautiful again.

"You know," I said, "it's not like we have to tell anybody what really happened. We can just tell the old guys that the fishing was lousy, that we ran through the food faster than we planned, and that the Glucotron started going haywire. So, we decided to come back early."

"They'll never believe us."

"They would if we just picked up some grub and the spare Glucotron and then went back out for a couple of days."

He turned to look at me. "You'd do that just to get me out of a fight with Dad and *the Mom*?"

"Well, if it's a big deal for you. Hell, it wouldn't be so bad to go fishing for another couple of days."

He laughed. "God, you really are turning into Joe Nature, aren't you?"

"Don't get carried away, Charlie. I'm just saying that it'd be all right to spend a little more time away from civilization."

He thought about it. "Yeah, I guess that wouldn't be too bad at that. But I don't think they'd believe us about the food. They'd figure something happened."

"Nah, they're always joking about how much teen-agers eat."

"How much you eat, maybe."

"Hey, give me some slack or forget it."

He laughed. "Well, maybe we could pull it off. I won't even mention the Glucotron, just get the spare out of the trunk."

"One thing. I've got to have a couple of cheese-burgers and some fries before we do the nature thing again, man."

"Me, too. So, is that the plan, then?"

"Suits me. But I want you to know that I'm only suffering for your sake."

"Oh, nice guy. You must be taking guilt-trip lessons from *the Mom.*"

We'd been making good speed, but the wind picked up as the sun warmed the water. Every now and then, I shaded my eyes against the glare to scan the waters to the north and west, hoping to pick out the silver glint of canoes. But like all the days before, our only companions were the gulls drifting on the wind currents and the loons diving and calling across the blue waters that I'd dreamed about in the night — waters cold blue all the way to the Arctic, where the aurora lit night skies with twisting bands of color. The memory of that dream gave me a chill of pleasure. God, I'd better watch out, or this Joe Nature thing might really get out of hand.

By the time we reached the portage to Hog Snout, I'd calculated and recalculated how long it would take us to get across the three lakes between Talking Bird and Cant Hook. But no matter how I figured, it didn't look good for making it that night. Randy must have been thinking the same thing, because when we landed at the head of the trail, he said, "Think maybe we should try the river? We're going to burn a lot of time carrying everything across this portage."

I looked down the narrow, rocky trail and then at the swift, deep river running beside it. From where we stood, the river looked a hell of a lot more attractive. "I don't know," I said. "I would, except that these damned Roman numerals on the map still bother me. I mean, just how bad is a class one or a class two rapids?"

"I guess we could walk down the trail a ways and check them out."

"That's not going to work. The trail cuts away from the river to take the shortest way to Hog Snout." I showed him on the map.

"Let's compromise then," he said. "We'll go slow and just walk it along the shore if we run into trouble. That should be safe enough."

I shrugged. "Okay, it's your call."

"Uh-uh, we make the call together or we don't go at all. And that is definitely not an option."

"All right. Let's give it a try."

We shoved off and paddled cautiously downstream. The river slipped smooth and deep through the overhanging trees with only the occasional V-shaped slick on the water showing where a boulder lay just beneath the surface. Dad had drummed the principles for spotting rocks into my head, even as he'd told me to avoid anything that looked even vaguely like a rapids: upstream V, boulder at the point; downstream V, clear sailing between rocks.

The river was picking up speed as it narrowed toward a bend to the right. In the bow, Randy said, "Do you hear something?"

I listened and picked up a sound like a distant freight train. I edged the canoe a little closer to the left shore, but as we nosed into the bend, the current suddenly got a lot stronger, grabbing the canoe and shoving us back into the middle of the stream. Randy let out a yelp and lifted a hand to point ahead, and I felt my stomach flip over as the current swept us clear of the bend, revealing white water breaking across the river from shore to shore. It was too late to make it to either side, and I searched desperately for a V of black water that would point the way downstream. In the bow, Randy seemed paralyzed, his paddle forgotten across his knees and his body bent forward like he was staring at death itself. "Keep paddling," I shouted. "I think I see a way through." His paddle came up and he started paddling for all he was worth.

I didn't have a lot of time to think about steering strokes, but somehow I managed to dodge the rocks at the head of the rapids before cutting into a rushing V of black water that dipped like a slide as the river plunged over a ledge. Sonia, goddamn it! Where are you now? You'd love this shit! The bow dropped and bucked up, water exploding around Randy and splashing in to soak the packs. We hit a rock that thumped the canoe like a drum and knocked us sideways so that for an instant I thought we were going over before my hands snapped the bow straight with a hard reverse sweep. And then, miraculously, we were free of the rapids and coasting in quiet water.

I turned to look back. The rapids seemed smaller, almost insignificant: a froth of white water with a clear, smooth path of black sliding over the almost invisible ledge that had seemed like the end of the world when we'd hit it.

Randy was laughing. "Way to go, partner. You got us through. God, that was a hell of a ride."

"It doesn't look half so bad from here. See that black-water V just to the left of that rock below the ledge? If I'd cut into that, we wouldn't have hit anything."

"Well, you did okay."

"We both did."

"Okay, we both did. How many more do we have like that?"

I glanced downstream, saw nothing to worry about, and got out the map. "That was a class one. The next is a class two, and then there's another class one just before we come out on Hog Snout."

"Well, the ones aren't going to get us, and we should be able to do the two if it's only a little tougher."

I felt an odd exhilaration, but caution got the better of it. "Maybe, but I don't think we should take a chance without looking it over first."

We maneuvered through two more bends, dodging a few rocks, the sound of the downstream rapids coming louder. Both sides of the river were thick with spruce and pine, and I was getting very nervous about finding a place to land when the river suddenly broadened, and we got our first look at the class two. "It doesn't look too bad," Randy shouted over the roar. "Not much worse than the first one."

I looked ahead for any swirl marking rock just below the surface and then stood shakily for a look. No, it didn't look too bad — not that I'd ever call anything wet, loud, and scary good — and I thought I saw a clear path through the rocks. I sat, wishing that I could have a quiet minute on shore to be sure, and yelled, "Okay, I've got the way picked out."

In those few seconds standing, I'd counted two drops this time, but I figured that as long as I didn't let the canoe swing broadside to the current, we'd have a decent chance of staying upright and afloat. We came between a couple of boulders and dipped down and up through the first drop. "Rock," Randy screamed, "dead ahead." For a split second, my brain froze, but somehow my arms knew what to do, reaching the paddle parallel to the water and jamming it in for a hard sweep that snapped the bow to the left. I had a brief glimpse of a jagged rock sliding past the bow, and then my arms reversed the sweep, kicking the stern to the left so that the rock swept past no more than an inch from the stern. We hit the second drop and again the bow bucked down and up. I tried to focus on the path ahead through the spray. And there it was, just to the left between a rock that barely broke the surface and another as high as my head. It seemed an impossible cut, but again my arms were doing the thinking. A sweep stuck the bow into the V of black water. Randy reached out to push off on the rock, but my reverse sweep straightened us so that we slid through with only a couple of seconds of grating against the big rock. And once again we were clear and coasting.

For a second, I couldn't tell if Randy was happy or hysterical. For that matter, I couldn't tell about my own laughter. I turned to look upstream, and what we'd been through no longer seemed so wild. "Now that was a ride," Randy said. "One class two, that's enough for me. At least for today."

"Me, too. Let's take a break."

We beached the canoe, careful to tie it up before worrying about anything else. I got out the map and tried to figure out how far we had to go to the lake. Something about the distances didn't quite make sense. "What's bothering you?" he asked.

"Nothing. Just trying to figure out exactly where we are."

"Well, one easy rapids to go, that's all I care about. I don't see why they even bother to mark those class ones. Don't seem worth mentioning once you've done a class two."

"Right," I said sarcastically. "Maybe you want to paddle stern this time."

"Nah, you're getting it down." He looked at the reading on the Glucotron. "Shit, this thing is really screwed. I'm hungry, I'm thirsty, and this thing is still reading high." He popped a candy in his mouth and offered the box to me.

"No, thanks. I've already had my quota for the day." He opened his mouth, but I interrupted. "Don't start on me. I'm not sacrificing; I'm just counting on one hell of a pig-out tonight."

"Me, too. You really think we can make it today?"

"Yeah, I'm starting to think so. Skipping this portage saves us a couple of hours. One more class one and we're on ol' Hog Snout. It should be pretty smooth sailing after that." I hesitated. "I just wish the river matched the map a little better. . . ."

He moved closer for a look. "I don't get the problem."

I shrugged. "It just doesn't seem like we could have come this far yet."

"We were moving pretty fast in those rapids. Come on, let's get going. I don't want to run out of daylight within smelling distance of those burgers."

I folded the map unwillingly. "It's just funny that — "

"Mark, stop worrying. We're pros now. Let's go."

I shrugged. "Okay."

We shoved off and almost immediately started hearing the roar of the next rapids. And it was louder this time, which didn't make sense. What the hell was going on? Was the map wrong, or was I? In the bow, Randy was horsing around, waving his paddle forward in a charge motion every few strokes, but my gut was telling me that something didn't compute and that I'd better figure out what in one hell of a hurry. Around the bend ahead, the roar grew so that it seemed about to swallow the world. Randy stopped screwing around and sat with his paddle across his thighs. Suddenly, the circuits snapped together in my brain and I had the answer: My God, that first rapids hadn't been a class one; it'd been something too insignificant to mark on the map at all! And, so surprise, surprise, stupid, you're about to be killed. "Backwater!" I screamed. "This is the class two!"

But it was too late; the current grabbed us like a giant hand and propelled us around the bend in a rush. On the far side, the river tumbled into a chasm between high walls. And there was no time for yelling or praying or doing anything but trying to stay alive in the roar of white water against black boulders. The first drop came at us so fast that I never had a chance to pick a course, and all I could do was hold the bow straight so that we didn't roll. The bow seemed to run straight into thin air, dropped, hit water hard as concrete, bucked up, and slammed head on into a rock breaking just above the torrent over the ledge. A foot or two either way, and we would have made it, but the impact knocked Randy headfirst into the river, his canoe paddle flying high over the water. I never saw it land, as the canoe swung broadside to the current. I hung on for a desperate second, trying to fight the river, and then dove free as the rush of water over the ledge flipped the canoe out from under me. I was underwater and the current was black and cold and very strong, and I could only go with it, pulling my knees up and hunching my shoulders, as I tried to shield my face with my hands. I felt the river drop under me, and I washed over a second ledge, the current plunging me deep on the other side, swirling, and for just an instant easing its grip on me. I unfolded then and struck out for the shore with everything I had. I surfaced in a pool hollowed out of the rocky shoreline below the rapids, grabbed an overhanging branch, and managed to drag myself onto the bank.

Something snagged my foot as I sprawled there, still clinging to the branch. I kicked at it, a fleeting image of something scaly with very sharp teeth flashing in my head. I looked, saw one of the sleeping bags unfurling from its stuff sack as the current swept it past, and lunged for it, just managing to catch a corner. The bag must have weighed twenty pounds, but I managed to pull it back toward me as the branch creaked against my weight. It held and I collapsed backward onto the bank with the bag hugged to my chest.

Shit. Where was Randy? I sat up, looking about wildly. But the river had swallowed him, the canoe, the packs, and every bit of evidence that he'd ever existed. Swallowed everything except me and the soggy sleeping bag. "Randy," I screamed, and then screamed his name again and again, because he couldn't be dead, because he wouldn't leave me out here all alone. No, if he just heard me one time, he'd come up from the bottom, come to the surface dazed but still alive. And then we'd be okay, even if the river kept everything else when it let us go.

My shouts came back to me, bouncing off the trees, the rocks, and the river. And when I heard my own name, at first I didn't believe, thinking it only my imagination or a trick of the echo. But it made me pause to listen and this time I heard. "I'm over here, Mark! For God's sake, stop bleating like . . ." The roar of the river carried away the rest of his words, leaving me still not quite ready to believe what I could not see. And then, at last, I spotted him perched on a boulder far upstream, the water over the big ledge tumbling around him.

For a moment, I felt like I was going to be sick, but I fought it back. "What'd you say?" I yelled.

"I said, 'Stop bleating like a sick goat.' I kept yelling but you wouldn't listen."

"Are you okay?"

"Yes. Are you?"

"I'm alive. Just a minute, I'll come closer."

I worked upstream until I was nearly opposite him. "Where's the canoe?" I shouted.

He gestured toward a spot beyond his boulder. "It's over here. Caught between a couple of rocks."

"Upside down?"

"No, it's right side up, but it's half full of water. The packs are gone. What do we do now?"

Damned good question, Charlie. "I've got one of

the sleeping bags. We'd better try to find the other stuff before it washes down to the lake. We'll worry about the canoe after that. Can you get to the other side?"

He turned and studied the river for a minute. "Yeah, I can make it."

"Good. I'll look along this side."

I made my way downstream, wading through the shallows when the overhanging trees made it impossible to walk on the shore. We'd screwed up big, but I couldn't waste any time getting mad at myself just yet. To hell with the sleeping bags and the tent. We needed the food pack and the paddles. God, if nothing else, we had to find the paddles. And Randy's diabetes kit. With those, we could still make it.

I found the food pack hung up on the branches of a deadhead bobbing up and down in the current. I waded out, the current tugging at my legs, and retrieved it. Empty. Not even a granola bar in a side pocket. I tossed it on the shore beside the sleeping bag.

From the opposite shore, Randy yelled, "I've got one of the paddles."

I waved. "Good. But one's not enough. We've got to find the other one."

Downstream, I spotted a plastic bag washed up against a rock. What the hell could that be? I waded out and got it. The bag of dehydrated potatoes and onions. Oh, great. We didn't have anything to cook them in, but God knows we had enough water to soak them. I went back for the sleeping bag and the empty pack and crossed to Randy's side as he waded around the bend. "One paddle, a poncho, one life preserver, and the canteen," he called.

I held up the plastic bag. "I found the potatoes and the food pack. The pack's empty."

His shoulders slumped. "No IJ?"

"Nope. You had it in the pack, huh?"

"Yeah, I stuck it in there for safekeeping just before we shoved off to try the river."

"I don't imagine it'd float."

He shook his head. "No, it would've gone down like a rock. With the Glucotron and the IJ, it's pretty heavy."

I bit my lip. "How long can you go without IJ?"

"I'm not sure. What do you think the chances are of finding it?"

I looked upstream at the frothing white water below the rapids. Not a chance in hell, Charlie. "Not good, but I guess we can try. Are you gonna be okay until tonight if we don't find it? Maybe even tomorrow morning."

"Yeah, I guess," he said, not looking at me.

"Tell me the truth; I need to know."

"Well, I'm going to have to be, huh? I mean, what other choice have I got?"

"Hey, don't get defensive. I'm just worried."

"Well, don't worry about me. Worry about the canoe, because we are definitely not going to make it unless we get it off those rocks."

"Okay, let's go get it. I'll walk in the water, you try the shore again. Maybe we'll find something."

Wading in midstream, I fell twice on the slippery

rocks, giving my knee a good bang the second time, but I kept going, hoping that by some freak chance I'd stumble on the diabetes kit or at least spot the missing canoe paddle hung up on a rock or a log. No luck, and I had to give up when the current got too strong below the rapids.

I had my first good look at the canoe when I joined Randy on the shore. It was lodged between two rocks, its bow awash and its stern in the air. The heavy current coming over the ledge broke against the stern, pounding the aluminum hull like a bass drum. "It's going to be a bitch getting it off," Randy said.

"You've got that right." I sat down on the shore and began emptying my pockets. "What do you have left?"

We piled the little we still had in a mound. I had my jackknife, the waterproof container of matches, a bottle of bug repellent, the compass from around my neck, and a ball of aluminum foil from what I couldn't remember. Randy contributed his tin of butterscotch candy, a couple of steel sinkers, and a spool of fishing line. All the rest was garbage: pocket change, our fishing licenses, a soaked book of matches, and a couple of equally worthless five-dollar bills. I looked at him. "Is that all you carry in your pockets?"

"I usually carry things in my kit. I don't like a lot of stuff in my pockets."

"Like a woman and her purse," I said sarcastically.

He flared. "Hey, screw you, man. I wasn't the one who misread the map."

"And I wasn't the one who suggested that we try this damned river."

"We made that call together. You know that. And

you're not the one who's going to die if we don't make it out of here." The reply I was about to make froze in my throat. He sat back on his heels and looked away. "Shit. I wasn't going to say that."

After a minute, I said, "I'm sorry. That was a stupid crack. You're right, I screwed up."

"No, we did it together. That's the deal, remember? Everything together, no matter how it goes." I nodded, not looking at him. Yeah, that's what we'd agreed. But I knew it was still my fault more than his. Joe Nature. Joe Stupid was more like it. "Let's go get the canoe," Randy said.

We stripped off our shirts and gazed at the fast water. "Maybe we ought to hold on to a belt," I said. "That way if one of us slips, the other might be able to keep him from washing downstream."

"Okay," he said. "Might as well use yours. It's longer by a foot or two."

I glanced at him. "You never ease up, do you?"

"Just trying to find a little humor in a disaster. Like you did with the bear."

I grunted sourly and pulled my belt off. We waded into the waist-deep water, holding on to either end of the belt. It was impossible to stand upright, and we had to lean into the current as we edged sideways toward the big boulder where Randy had perched after getting thrown from the canoe. The back of my pants filled with water and the waist started slipping down over my ass. Oh, great.

Just short of the boulder, Randy stumbled. I tried to hold him, but lost my grip on the belt. He toppled backward with a splash and came to the surface paddling like crazy. I managed to make it the last few feet to the boulder and braced my back against it. Randy got into the eddy below it, staggered to his feet, and managed to stumble within reach. I grabbed his hand and pulled him the rest of the way.

"Thanks," he panted. "I don't think I'm going to worry about boiling the water anymore. I've swallowed so much duck and beaver shit by this time, I don't think it'll matter."

"Me, too. I just hope we don't get the runs before we get back to the resort. Ready?"

"Yeah. Give me a boost." I got my hand under his butt. "Don't get too friendly," he said.

"Shut up," I said. "This is serious. Okay, one, two, three!" I pushed and he scrambled up the side of the boulder. He turned, got his feet braced, and reached for my hand. I took it, found a toehold, and lunged upward, the rock scraping against my bare chest as he leaned back.

We sat resting for a minute atop the boulder, the canoe barely three yards away. "I don't imagine you thought to bring my belt with you," I said.

"Sorry, it's back there somewhere."

"Great. Just great."

He peered downstream. "Maybe it'll float — "

"Forget it. We've got more important things to worry about. Okay, here's what I think we ought to do. . . ." I explained.

"No simpler way, huh?"

"Not unless you can think of one."

"No, that's better than anything I can think of."

"Well, let's do it then."

I edged myself over the upstream side of the boulder, gauged the distance, and dropped into the water. The current grabbed me, pulling me downstream feetfirst between the boulder and the nearer of the two rocks holding the canoe. I aimed my feet at the rock, hit it, and grabbed the gunwale of the canoe. The canoe bucked with the current, but I managed to keep hold as I worked my way to the bow, untied the rope, and then edged back to the stern, holding the rope in my teeth. I retied it there, balled up the trailing end, and threw it to Randy. "Okay, hang on tight," I yelled. "Once it comes loose, it's gonna try like hell to get away."

"I'll hold it," he called, took a turn of the rope around his leg, and leaned back, holding on with both hands.

I worked my way to the forward thwart, took a good hold, and heaved back against the current. The canoe budged a bare three inches before the current slammed it back between the rocks. Okay, you son of a bitch. I braced one foot against the rock and threw my weight back as hard as I could.

Ever notice how most things take three tries, maybe five for really stupid people like me? After a while, you almost start to expect the first two — or four — tries to fail. Not this time. The bow came out from between the rocks so suddenly that I lost my balance. The stern dropped with a splat and all the water in the bow rushed aft. I was still clutching the thwart with one hand as I tried to get my balance, but the bow snapped to the right and knocked me off my feet. The weight of the canoe was more than Randy could handle alone, and that's when some elementary physics came into play big time. Or, at least I guess that's what you'd use to figure out just exactly how fast a hundred-and-forty-pound kid is going to get yanked off a boulder when he's got one end of a rope wrapped around his leg and the other end tied to a runaway canoe. Fast and with a minimum of form. Randy tumbled, hitting the water head over heels. The canoe wallowed, fighting like some huge fish to break free of my one-handed grip. And I knew, in one of those sudden flash-camera certainties that even really stupid people have once in a while, that if I didn't hold on, the canoe would drag him downstream underwater and kill him against the rocks. I threw my weight against the side of the canoe, pinning it to the nearer of the two rocks. Randy thrashed to the surface, his face contorted with pain. "Christ, I can't get the rope off my leg!"

"Help me hold the canoe," I yelled. "We've got to do that first." The current threw us together. Sobbing with the pain, he leaned hard against the canoe. "Just hold on," I gasped, got a better hold, and braced my feet against the slippery rocks deep in the swirling current. "Okay, I've got it. But get the rope off fast; I can't hold it for long."

He went underwater for what seemed like forever as my shoulders and legs screamed with the effort. Finally, he shot to the surface. "It's off!"

"Okay, watch yourself. I'm letting it go. One, two, three . . . Now!" He plunged toward the boulder, and I let go, trying to throw myself clear as the canoe shot from under my hands, the stern snapping left and catching me a nasty swat across the back.

Whatever hope I'd had that we might recover the

canoe downstream and get out of the wilderness afloat evaporated in the next thirty seconds. The canoe bounced off half a dozen rocks, the dull booming coming to us over the roar of the rapids, and then swung sideways across the current, rolled, and tilted out of the water on its side for the instant it took the river to drive it into a huge rock. We heard the snapping of seams and the shriek of twisting aluminum as water plowed into bow and stern, breaking the canoe's back against the rock. The canoe twisted away with a final screech of metal on stone, wobbled clear of the rapids into the smooth water below, and sank.

CHAPTER EIGHT

The rope on the stern trailed in the water as the canoe bobbed along the bottom on its slow way toward the last rapids and the lake beyond. We towed it to the side of the river to examine the damage. The hull was bent like a banana, the long seam along the keel cracked half the canoe's length. "It's finished," I said. "Completely."

Randy nodded. "No argument there." For a couple of minutes, we just stood staring at the damage, then Randy seemed to shake himself. "Well, I guess we won't be able to hide this one from the old guys and *the Moms*. Not that it's the most important thing in my life right now."

"Yeah, we've got one or two more important things to worry about."

"Just a couple. So what do we do now?"

"I guess there's a chance we'll spot somebody on Hog Snout or one of the other lakes."

"Suppose we don't. How long is it going to take us to walk out?"

I hesitated. "I'm not sure. As the crow flies, it's not

much more than twenty miles. Trouble is, we aren't crows."

"No map, huh?"

"Not unless we spot it floating on the lake. But I think I've got the picture pretty well in my head, and we've still got the compass. If we keep in sight of water, we won't get lost. We won't have much to carry, anyway."

He snorted. "That's the understatement of the year." He stared at the river again. "If I hadn't skipped my morning shot, I wouldn't worry so much. But the way it is, we'd better get moving. What time is it, anyway?"

I glanced at my watch, noticing for the first time the cracked crystal and the blank face. "No telling from my watch." I showed it to him.

"These sports watches ain't exactly what they're cracked up to be."

"So to speak," I said. Together we stared at the sun. "So what do you think, Charlie?"

"Indian timekeeping's your department, but I'd guess about one."

"Yeah, that's about what I thought." I took off the watch and tossed it beside the rest of the stuff we'd scrounged from the river. Randy pulled out the wad of worthless junk we'd screened from our pockets. He folded the two five-dollar bills and put them back in his pocket. "I'll save these to buy us burgers and fries at the resort, because I don't plan on dying out here, no matter what I said before." He sat, took off his boots, and wrung the water out of his socks. I did the same. "God, I wish I had a pair of dry socks," he said. "This isn't gonna be comfortable. So, what else is worth taking?"

"I guess we can eat those dried onions and potatoes raw. Or at least you can."

"My favorite. How about the sleeping bag?"

"It weighs a ton, but we're going to need it if we don't get out until tomorrow. We can dry it by the fire tonight, then at least one of us can sleep warm."

"We can unzip it. That way it'll stretch over both of us."

"Maybe, but I'm not sure I'm feeling that friendly just yet."

We wrung the water out of the bag and shoved it into the food pack along with the few other things worth saving. I hiked up my jeans. "Just let me cut a piece of the rope. If we do die out here, I don't want to be found with my pants falling down."

"You are looking skinnier. Starvation agrees with you."

"Just keep joking. We're going to need a lot of humor from here on in. Might as well fill the canteen from the river. We're not going to have time to boil any water until tonight."

I untied the rope from the canoe, cut a length to knot around my waist, and shoved the rest in the pack. We started off, but I had a small idea then, and returned to the pile of junk to retrieve the ball of aluminum foil. No frying pan, but this might do.

Above the last rapids, we stumbled onto a deer trail, following it through the woods until it swung back to the river below the white water. We turned together to look upstream. "Isn't that the pits?" Randy said. "Hell, that one looks easier than any of them."

"Yeah," I said. "If we'd just carried the canoe around the big one, we could have made it no sweat."

We were wasting time, but we stood there for a few more minutes, as if we both sensed that when we turned our back on the river, we would somehow be leaving more behind than just the scene of our disaster. Randy took a long swallow from the canteen. "You know, we never named the canoe. Somehow that makes me feel bad. Like we should have given it a little respect before we wrecked it."

"Yeah," I said, "it was a pretty good boat." I hiked up the pack and turned to follow the river to the shore of Hog Snout.

Something green billowed in the slight chop fifty or sixty yards offshore. "What is it?" Randy asked.

"The other poncho, I think."

"Worth going after?"

I hesitated, glancing at the sky. "I guess. It's pretty clear now, but we could get rain later on."

"I'll go. You've done most of the swimming so far."

I was about to say, "Be my guest," but instead I said, "No. As you keep pointing out, I'm the one with fat to spare."

He started to protest, but checked himself. "Yeah, I guess you're right. Hey, but it's my treat for the cheeseburgers when we get to the resort."

"I'll remember that." I stripped naked and waded in. For some reason, the water seemed colder than ever this time, and my feet were numb by the time I reached the poncho. I grabbed it, rolled the flopping SOB into a ball, and stroked back in. "God, where's the fire this time?" I chattered.

"Sorry, I didn't think I should waste a match. We've only got half a dozen left in that waterproof container of yours."

"Only half a dozen?"

"Yeah, I checked while you were taking your dip."

"Shit, I never thought to refill it. What a stupid, damned move."

He shrugged. "Another thing to remember for next time. That and the bear cable for the packs."

"Yeah, next time." I swore again and started pulling on my clothes.

"Which way now?"

I gestured toward the east. "It's shorter around this side, I think. Not a lot, but a little."

"Lead on."

Another bum decision. We crossed the portage trail we should have taken that eternity ago when we'd decided to shoot the rapids. Beyond the foot of the trail, the trees grew right down to the edge of the lake, and we had to fight our way through brush and over deadfalls. I kept hoping for higher ground, but then we hit a swamp so thick that after two flailing attempts, the mud and the bugs drove us back.

We rested at the edge of the swamp. I was breathing hard, but Randy was actually panting. "How you doing?" I asked.

"Just a little winded. Don't worry, I'm okay." He got up to take a whiz.

"Jeez, don't you ever get empty? That's about the fourth time you've taken a leak in the last hour."

He shrugged. "Sometimes the Big D does that to me. What do we do now?"

I looked at the sun. Going on three o'clock, I guessed. "We're going to have to go back and try to get around the lake to the west. It's that or swim across. And believe me, the water's too damned cold for that." I got up and started back the way we'd come. Randy hesitated a moment and then followed.

I'd been putting off getting the details, but I knew it was time to start asking questions. Start slow, I thought. "So, uh, how do you figure your blood's doing?"

He waited so long to reply that I thought he hadn't heard the question. "I'm not sure. I thought the Glucotron was screwed up when it said I was so high, but now I'm beginning to wonder."

"How come?"

"Well, stress can knock the readings all out of whack sometimes."

"You think that's what's happened now?"

"Maybe. It's hard to know what's going on for sure."

I concentrated, trying to get all the highs and lows straight. "Wait a second. If you're low, you need food. If you're high, you need IJ. You don't have either, so aren't you going to balance out?" I looked at him hopefully. "At least for a while?"

He grimaced. "It's not that simple. Somewhere along the line, my body's gonna start burning fat for energy. And that's going to pump acids into my system. They're called ketones or keotones, I don't remember for sure, but they're not good."

"What do you mean, 'not good'?"

"Poisonous."

I felt suddenly cold. "How poisonous?"

"I don't know. I've never really worried about them before. But I don't think they're anything to mess with."

"You think that's happening to you now?"

"No, not quite yet. But I sure wish to hell I'd taken my shot this morning. The way things are, I'd better get a regular meal and some IJ by tomorrow morning sometime. Tonight would be better."

I glanced at the sun again. Well, you can forget tonight, Charlie.

We crossed the portage trail and reached the river again, took off our boots and socks, and waded across. Along the west side of Hog Snout, the walking got easier, and we made better time. Then we hit bog again. We tried a couple of different routes before facing up to the fact that one way or another, we were going to have to slog our way through. We found a couple of thick branches to prod the ground ahead and trimmed them with my knife.

"There isn't anything nasty like quicksand around here, is there?" Randy asked.

"God, I don't think so. Nobody ever mentioned it."

"Yeah, but nobody's ever been stupid enough to try walking up here. Everybody sticks to the water. Just like the Indians did."

He was probably right. In all the thousands of years since the last Ice Age, we might well be the first fools to try walking around Hog Snout Lake. At least in the summertime. "Well," I said, "if you start getting sucked down, I'll try to pull you out with my stick. But don't expect me to dive in after you."

"Yeah. Same for me. Can I have your girl if you don't make it?"

"I guess if she's willing. But I expect her to become a nun if I don't come back."

He snorted. "You wish. I thought you were worried that she wouldn't wait this long."

I was. Or at least I had been before a few more important things had started to worry me. "Nah, I'm not worried anymore. When she sees how tan and thin I am after this trip, she'll never be able to resist."

"And lumpy. There's a mosquito doing a Dracula number on your neck right now."

I slapped it, my palm coming away sticky with blood. "Well, let's give it another try. I'm not getting back to her any faster this way."

We went into the swamp, the mosquitoes and black-flies sticking to us in swarms. The black mud oozed over the tops of our boots and made an obscene sucking sound every time we lifted a foot. I fell once and Randy fell twice, our arms going into the muck nearly to the elbows and coating us with the stench of a thousand years of rotting vegetation.

We were two pretty sorry-looking and very bad-smelling campers by the time we made it to the far side of the swamp. On dry ground at the lake's edge, I shrugged out of the pack and tried to scrape off as much of the mud as I could. Randy sat and took off his boots. His face looked flushed to me, but maybe that was just my imagination. "I'm getting a blister from these wet socks," he said.

I waved away a few dozen blackflies trying to set up housekeeping in my ears. "Yeah, I'm getting one, too. How much longer do you think you can keep going?"

"As long as you can, partner," he snapped.

I shrugged. "I'd hang it up right here if I had my choice, but we've still got daylight." I got out the repellent, eyeballed the level in the bottle, and then shook a few drops onto a palm. I tossed the bottle to him.

"Thanks. So where do you figure we are?"

"I think we're nearly to the western tip of the lake. The shoreline should swing back east pretty quick to hit the river draining into Black Dan."

"What then?"

"Well, if we're lucky, maybe we'll spot somebody on Black Dan. If not, we'll try going around the western side. If the walking doesn't get too bad, we should make it halfway around by dark."

"How far will we be then?"

I hesitated. "Maybe halfway to Cant Hook."

"That's all, huh?"

" 'Fraid so."

"You're sure?"

"Yeah."

"Shit. I thought we'd get farther today."

"So did I. But maybe we've seen the worst."

He hesitated. "No offense, partner, but do you suppose the Mountain Man and Bob the Nazi would have figured out an easier way to do this?"

I snorted. "Well, the Mountain Man probably could

have thrown together a birchbark canoe in a couple of hours. Or maybe Bob would just have ordered the water to freeze so they could walk across."

"Come on, that's a serious question."

"Well, I don't know what they would have done! They didn't screw up. Guys like them never screw up!" I turned away, surprised to find angry tears welling in my eyes. Bob. God, he was going to have a good time with this.

Randy said quietly, "I was just wondering if they would have tried to get out overland. You know, followed a straight line with the compass until they hit a road. Be faster than following the shore."

I got a grip. "Maybe they would have. But I'm just not that good with a compass. You looked at the map. There is a hell of a lot of country out there. Even if we kept going in a straight line, it might be days before we hit a road. At least this way we pretty much know where we are and where we've got to go."

"Yeah, I guess you're right." He stood, working his toes in his wet boots. "Well, I guess we've got some tracks to make, then."

I tried a joke. "Yeah, the Big S is starting to get to me." He gave me a quizzical look. "Starvation," I said. "I'm hungry."

"Yeah, me, too. Let me take a whiz, and then we'll get another mile toward those cheeseburgers."

While he was draining his bladder again, I reached for the canteen. Nearly empty again — no wonder he was always stopping to take another leak. I swept away some leaves and junk on the surface of the lake and filled it.

"I'm ready," Randy said. "Lead the way, Joe Nature."

"Why don't you give that a rest?" I said.

"Oh. Sure," he said.

I shrugged into the pack, cursing the wet sleeping bag that was dripping water down into my pants, and led the way to the west.

We had easier going as we got around the end of the lake and followed the southern shore back to the east. A breeze was coming off the lake, driving the bugs back into the brush, and the walking was almost pleasant except that now I had time to think. All afternoon, I'd been trying not to think about Dad and Mom and Bob, and how they were going to react to the mess I'd made of things this time.

Dad would be disgusted. Just plain, flat disgusted. He'd blast me once, and then go into a long simmer that might last weeks or months or maybe forever. Back home I'd get no slack. He'd tell me what to do, when to do it, and stay on me until it was done. And sooner or later, we'd both start counting the days until I graduated and we could get free of each other for good.

But even Dad's reaction didn't scare me as much as Mom's. And that was because she wouldn't get mad enough. Somehow, I'd always been a disappointment to her. Never as good as Bob, never worth really getting mad at, since it couldn't do any good. She'd lay a lot of the blame on Dad and then write a letter to Bob about how she didn't know what she was going to do with me. And, God, I didn't know what I was going to do with me, either. Never had, probably never would. I felt tears well in my eyes and brushed them away quickly so that Randy wouldn't see. But he was walking with his head down, his gaze fixed dully on the ground, and hadn't noticed.

Figuring Bob was simple. So simple that I could imagine word for word the letter he'd send me. He'd review the story as he'd heard it from Mom, bashing me with sledgehammer sarcasm for every bad move I'd made. And when I was reduced to a bloody pulp, he'd lay out the program for making me into a man: "Now, Mark, I assume that you don't want to continue this way. No one with any self-respect would, after all the grief and worry you've caused Dad and especially Mom. So, let's get your act together. Nobody's going to expect miracles. Just start with the small things: Get your hair cut, shine your shoes, and wear something other than jeans and ratty sweatshirts. Next, make out a schedule. . . ."

And blah and blah and blah, summed up more or less as: "Get your weight down, your grades up, cut loose your scummy friends, help Mom with the twins, and at least *try* to make Dad and me proud of you." And at the end of reading his letter, I'd feel like shit. Because I'd know that a lot more than half of what he said was true. And, that no matter what I did, I'd never manage to measure up by even half of what I should.

By the time we reached the river flowing from Hog Snout into Black Dan, my stomach was complaining that it'd missed another meal. We rested on the bank, cooling our blistered feet in the slow water. "Hell," Randy said. "After the last one, I wouldn't even call this a river. It's more like that channel we paddled through getting into Ax Handle. Not a single rapids. God, it would have been a piece of cake."

"Yeah," I said, "a piece of cake."

"Well, no use thinking about that. Let me take — "

"I know," I said. "Let you take a whiz, and we'll get going."

"Bother you, or something?" he snapped.

"Nope. I just keep wondering where you get it all." I unscrewed the top and dipped the canteen in the river. Okay, I thought, something's happening. Even as hard as we've been working, nobody empties a canteen three times in an afternoon. Let it ride. If this is the worst that happens, we'll be lucky.

He came back, sucking on one of his butterscotch candies. "Want one? I've still got half a dozen."

"No, I'm fine. Gonna put your boots back on, or are you going barefoot?"

He glanced down. "I knew I forgot something." He laughed, sounding more than a little odd, and suddenly bent forward clutching his stomach. I jumped up and reached for him, thinking he was about to pitch forward on his face, but he put out a hand to stop me. "No, I'm okay. Just a cramp."

I stood there, my hands still half raised, feeling both stupid and useless. "You sure?"

He straightened painfully. "Yeah. Just a cramp. Must have drunk too much of this beaver-shit water."

Well, I could believe that. I hesitated another moment and then bent to pick up the pack.

We followed the river down to the shore of Black Dan and climbed a low hill for a look at the lake. Nothing and nobody, just vacant water all the way to the distant shore, where I thought I could make out a break in the trees cut by the river flowing south into Big Carry. I swallowed my disappointment. "Well, let's hope there's good walking along the west side."

"Uh, partner. I've about had it. Let's camp and give 'er a go early."

I glanced at him, suddenly very mindful of the ache in my own legs and the raw spots the wet pack straps had rubbed on my shoulders. "Yeah, okay. It's going to be dark soon, and I want to get enough wood in so we can dry out the sleeping bag. But we're really gonna have to move it in the morning."

He was already sitting down, unlacing a boot, and didn't reply. Before I went to gather wood, I emptied most of the water from the canteen, carefully poured in the dehydrated potatoes and onions, and left them to soak. When I got back with an armload of branches, Randy was staring off across the lake, his mouth half open, a limp sock forgotten in his hand. My God, had he seen something? I dropped the wood and squinted across the lake turning golden in the setting sun. "What? Did you see a boat?"

"Huh?"

"A boat! Did you see a boat?"

"Uh-uh. I was watching a couple of those birds. You know, the black ones with the white bellies. Whatcha-callems."

"Loons?"

"Yeah, loons. They were going in and out of that yellow streak on the water. It was pretty."

I stared at him. "Hey, you okay?"

"Me? Yeah, I'm fine. Except my gut hurts. Want me to start the fire?"

"No. Just break up some kindling. I need to get another armload."

When I got back again, he was sitting just as I'd left him, staring at the lake with the branches untouched beside him. I made the fire, trying to get it going on a single match but messing up and needing to use two. I spread the wet sleeping bag out to dry and then went in search of some bigger sticks.

When I got back, he was stretched out on the bag. "Hey, partner," I said, "that's going to dry out a lot faster if you're not lying on it."

He looked at me uncomprehendingly for a moment and then pushed himself up on an elbow and felt the bag. "Yeah, it is wet, isn't it? When'd that happen?"

Was he putting me on? "When we dumped the canoe, remember?"

"Oh, yeah." He shook his head, as if to clear cobwebs. "I must be more tired than I thought. And hungry."

"Well, I'm putting supper on in a minute." I got the ball of aluminum foil out of the pack and unrolled it carefully. I drained the water from the canteen, shook the partially swollen onions and potatoes onto the foil, folded it, and put it in the coals. It'd work. Not well, but better than nothing.

Despite my very broad hint, Randy hadn't stirred from the sleeping bag. I pulled at an end. "Come on, move. I'm going to give this a shake." He moved and sat a couple of yards from the fire, staring dreamily at the foil envelope of potatoes and onions steaming in the coals. I shook the sleeping bag and spread it out to dry some more.

When I figured the potatoes and onions had cooked through, I wet my fingers and pulled the foil package out of the coals. I let it cool a couple of minutes and then unrolled the top. "Eat hearty," I said.

"Aren't you going to have some?"

"No, I'm fine."

"Liar." He ate, and the food seemed to help him focus. The glop looked terrible and probably tasted worse, but I had to hold myself back from taking a bite. Once I started, I'd elbow him out of the way to get the rest. He looked up and grinned. "Cheeseburgers for lunch tomorrow, huh?"

"You bet. Right now I'm trying to decide if I'm going to eat five or six."

"Have six. I'm buying." He ate the last few shreds of potato, crumpled up the foil, and sat back with a grunt of satisfaction. "That'll help. I was feeling a little spacey before supper."

"Well, I cooked, you can do the dishes."

He considered the ball of foil in his hand, and then flipped it into the coals. "Done."

I put some wood on the fire and then stretched out on an elbow, watching the flames. I was too tired to worry. Come morning, we'd both have some energy back. Cheeseburgers for lunch. I let my eyes close.

Randy bolted for the brush, and I heard him heave and then heave again. Oh, hell, I thought, sat up, and waited for him to get done blowing supper and all the food we had except for the few butterscotch candies in his tin. He came back from the bushes and slumped down by the fire. For a long minute, neither of us spoke. "I'm sorry," he said. "I guess the food would have done you more good."

"It's okay. I wasn't that hungry, anyway."

"Hey, don't lie to me, jerk! I can hear your stomach growling from here."

I shrugged. "I'm sorry. I just didn't want you to feel bad."

"Don't worry how the hell I feel, okay?"

"Okay," I said. I watched him; he didn't look good at all.

He put his chin on a knee and stared into the fire. "God, I hate people lying to me. Back when I was first in the hospital, the doctors and my dad kept telling me that diabetes wasn't so bad, that I could live just like anybody else as long as I took my shots. What a bunch of bullshit. *The Mom*'s been right all along. I can't." After a minute, he started to say more, but he got tangled up and just sat brooding by the fire. I figured he was getting ready to blow, and I closed my eyes, telling myself that I had to ignore it if he started in on me. But the next time I glanced at him, he was nodding off, the firelight glistening on his damp skin.

I hesitated, then asked, "How bad is this going to get?"

"What?"

"With you and the Big D. No IJ, no food. All that stuff."

He stared at me as if he didn't quite understand, then lifted his shoulders and let them drop. "I dunno. Maybe I'll feel better tomorrow."

"Maybe we ought to get some sleep."

"I'm okay. You go ahead."

"No, I'll sit with you for a while."

We sat by the fire for another ten or fifteen minutes. I tried to concentrate on the problems ahead, tried to think through our route again, but my eyelids kept falling. Randy started to slump over and I caught him. "Come on, cousin, let's turn in," I said.

I got him onto the sleeping bag and tried to help him off with his boots. But he shook me away, and I watched as he removed them with agonizing slowness. I used a few drops of the mosquito dope and handed him the bottle. "Better put some on," I said. "It's a long time until morning." He grunted, shook some on a palm, and let the bottle drop to the ground. I picked it up, closed the nozzle, and waited as he very slowly rubbed the dope on his face and hair. Finally, he rolled into the damp bag, his face away from me.

I wrapped the ponchos around me and got as comfortable as I could beside the fire. I closed my eyes, again trying to picture the map. In the morning, we'd have to make a choice whether to head east or west to get around Black Dan. We couldn't afford much more backtracking, and I tried to recall every bog and every contour line on the map.

Finally, when I was sure Randy was asleep, I reached over and zipped up the open side of the bag. It was the only thing I could think of to do for him.

CHAPTER NINE

A cold mist on my face woke me from unsettled dreams beside the dead ashes of the fire. I unrolled from the ponchos and sat up shivering in the gray light. I looked out over the lake, hoping for the silhouette of a fishing boat, but saw nothing except a pair of loons cruising far out on the oily gray water.

Randy lay in the sleeping bag, breathing heavily through his open mouth. I shook him. "Time to get moving, partner." I waited and then shook him again. "Hey, Randy, come on. It's daylight, and we've got miles to cover."

He seemed to come up from a long way down. He stared at me groggily, recognition faint in his dull eyes. "I'm up," he mumbled.

"No, you're not. Come on, sit up."

He sat up, looking around like he couldn't remember how he'd come to be sleeping without a tent or a canoe beside a lake in some godforsaken outback of Minnesota. He rubbed his face. "What's for breakfast?"

"Butterscotch candy. Hey, don't lie down on me

again. Come on. There are cheeseburgers waiting for us at the resort." I kicked at the remains of the fire, hoping for a coal or two that might help me get a quick fire going. Nothing, just cold ash.

Randy stumbled to his feet and wobbled off a few feet to take a whiz. "How you doing?" I asked.

"Okay, but I need some IJ. Where's my kit?" He started looking around.

"Hey, Randy, it's gone. Damn near everything's gone. That's the drill, remember. We're a couple of city kids lost in the wilderness and trying to get out before we starve to death."

"Oh, yeah. Wasn't thinking for a second there."

Well, start thinking, Charlie. I rolled up the sleeping bag and shoved it into the pack. At least today it'd be dry and light. "We can waste a match trying to get a fire going," I said. "But I figure we can get warm faster walking."

"Okay. Lead on."

I fastened the flap and swung the pack onto my shoulders. "This way then, partner," I said, and led the way west.

Randy fell in behind. "I dreamed about Indians," he said. "Must have been a couple dozen canoes of them out on the lake. Not this one, but the big one we were on the other day."

"Ax Handle."

"Right. Anyway, they were moving along just as easy as you like. Women in the front, men in the back. Kids and even a couple of dogs in the middle with the packs. It was pretty."

"Yeah, I'll bet. Sounds like a Remington."

"A what?"

"Nothing," I said. "Just an artist who painted stuff like that."

"Oh, yeah. I kinda know who you mean. Well, you ought to paint this picture. I'll tell you all about it when we get back."

"Sure, Charlie."

For the first hour or so, we had good walking, the best yet. But Randy lagged behind, stopping often to pee or to drink from the canteen. How much time before the Big D really started catching up with him? I didn't know and that scared the hell out of me.

I concentrated on the map in my head again. But no matter how many times I figured the distance covered and the distance to go, we weren't in good shape. Even if we could keep up yesterday's pace, we'd be hard put to make it to Cant Hook before late afternoon — and then only if we didn't have to do any backtracking.

Yet the more I thought about the map, the more I was sure I remembered a thin, dotted track circling northeast from near the resort almost to the edge of Big Carry. I was no expert on maps, but I was willing to bet that it was some kind of logging road or fire lane. And if that was true, maybe it wasn't such a crazy idea to try cutting across country. From the western edge of Black Dan, it couldn't be more than three or four miles almost due south to the road, maybe less. Hell, with a little luck, we could be at the resort by afternoon.

The shore was already edging around to the south and I paused to check the compass.

Behind me, Randy coughed, hacked, and spat. "You okay?" I asked.

"Yeah. Just a leaf or something in the water." He peered into the canteen.

"I've been thinking we might try cutting overland once we get to the western edge of the lake."

"Whatever you say, Joe."

"Okay, then. We'll do it." I had a surge of optimism as we started off again. Another half a mile, and we'd take the plunge into the woods. Three miles overland, and we'd come out on the logging road. Then a brisk walk to the resort, IJ, and cheeseburgers. It was going to work. I knew it. And maybe if I explained everything carefully to Dad, just maybe he wouldn't be so pissed after all. Overland with just a compass and a mental image of the map. A feat worthy of the Mountain Man.

The mist couldn't decide if it wanted to turn into drizzle or blow away in the breeze. So it stayed, hanging on the lake and woods as the shoreline turned boggy, forcing us inland until we could just make out the lake through the trees. And then we hit it: a swamp wider and deeper than anything we'd seen before. My heart fell into my shoes. Oh, shit. I dropped the pack. "Wait here," I said. Randy flopped down, leaned back against a tree, and closed his eyes.

I followed the edge of the swamp westward for two or three hundred yards, trying to find a path through to the south. But the swamp only got thicker. I retreated to a hillock, climbed it, and tried to get a look. Trees hid much of the view, but from what I could tell, the swampy land extended far to the southwest. Son of a bitch. We could follow the edge of the swamp and maybe get around it, but my gut told me that we couldn't risk going that far out of our way. Hell, we could miss the logging road entirely and wander for days before we stumbled onto a road or a house. And we didn't have days. Of that I was sure. I sat down with my head in my hands and tried to imagine what Dad, Uncle Jerry, Bob, or Pete would do. They'd know for sure, but I didn't. Come on, jerk, think!

But no matter how I sorted the options, it all came back to the map. I knew where the lakes were, but I could only guess what lay out there beyond the western edge of the swamp. I'd have to lead Randy back around the other side of Black Dan, then south around Big Carry, and finally down the river to Cant Hook. Maybe we'd get lucky and spot fishermen or canoers somewhere along the way. Otherwise, we'd just have to gut it out.

On the way back to where I'd left him, I got turned around and had to fight down panic. "Randy," I yelled, heard nothing, and yelled again. Nothing. Okay, stupid, calm down. Walk back to the edge of the swamp and follow it to the east. You've got to find him that way.

I almost missed him anyway, passing within twenty feet of him before he stretched and asked, "What were you yelling about?"

"I was trying to find you. Why didn't you answer?"

"I did."

"Couldn't have been very loud."

He shrugged. "You're here, aren't you?" He closed his eyes again.

I started to get mad, then said to hell with it. But I

wasn't leaving him again, that was for sure. "Well, we're screwed," I said. "We're going to have to go back and try the other side of the lake."

"What's gotta be, gotta be," he said, not opening his eyes.

He didn't get it: We'd already wasted two hours of daylight, and we'd burn at least another hour getting back to where we'd started. I reached out a hand to help him up. "Come on, we've got to move."

He opened his eyes, stared at my hand, and then closed them again. "You go ahead. I'm gonna rest here a few minutes."

"No way," I said, got his arm, and started pulling him up.

He groaned. "Slave driver. Okay, okay. Let go of the bod. I'm with you."

We started back, but what I'd figured might take us an hour turned into two. Randy seemed to have lost all sense of urgency, pausing every couple of hundred feet for a whiz, a drink, or just to stare at a bird or a tree. And no matter how much I bitched at him, it didn't do a damned bit of good.

We crossed the river between Hog Snout and Black Dan and began edging around the east side of the lake, keeping close to the shore where the walking was better. About noon, Randy started vomiting. I was a few yards ahead and turned to see him on his hands and knees, heaving up what seemed like gallons of water. I waited, feeling nauseous myself. Finally, he sat back on his haunches, tears streaming down his face. "Oh, God," he groaned, "that hurts."

"Let me get you some water." I went to take the

canteen from him to fill it at the lake. It was gone. "Randy, where's the canteen?"

"I don't know," he said. "Back there someplace. It was empty."

I stared at him, too stunned to speak. Any fool could see what was happening to him, but I still didn't want to believe it. Those keotones or ketones or whatever the hell they were called were poisoning him surer than hell. I'd seen it all morning in the darkening flush on his face and in how he never quite got his breath back when we stopped to rest. Now those acids were seeping into his brain, leaving him unable to make the simple connection between an empty canteen and filling it from the lake just a dozen yards to our right. "Wait here," I said. "Just rest a few minutes." I dropped the pack and hurried back along the way we'd come.

It took me twenty minutes to find the canteen, lying half hidden in some brush, and another ten to get back to Randy. He was curled up beside the pack, asleep. I filled the canteen at the water's edge. He wasn't going to make it unless I started getting tough with him. Maybe not even then. But if he was going to have any chance at all, I'd have to get him within sight of Cant Hook by evening. Then maybe I could leave him long enough to go get help. But I couldn't leave him here. No way.

I shook him, and he groaned. "Randy, get up. We've got to keep going." He rolled over and put his head on his arm. I shook him again. "Come on. Let's go."

"Go away," he mumbled.

I got my hands under his arms and pulled him into a sitting position against the pack. "Here, I brought

171

you some water." He took the canteen but let it fall into his lap. "Randy, take a drink and then let's get going."

He smiled, as if I had no more reality than whatever he'd been dreaming. "Nah, I'm gonna rest here a little while. You go ahead. I'll catch up later."

"You'll get lost."

He shook his head. "Nah, I'm just like an Indian. I'll track you through anything. You'll never get away." He smiled dreamily. "Yeah, Indians. That's what we need. Bunch of Indians to get us out of here. Take us in their canoes and dump us off home. Why don't you go find us some Indians?"

Before I could think better of it, I grabbed him by the front of the shirt and jerked him to his feet. "God-damn it, come on!"

"Hey, whatcha doin'?" he whined, trying to push me away.

I shook him. "Trying to save your life, damn it! Remember IJ, man? Well, you need it and you need it bad. So let's go get some." That seemed to get through. He stood wobbling for a minute, then took a deep, ragged breath, and seemed steadier. I let go of his shirt slowly. "You with me now?"

"Yeah, yeah. I'm with you. IJ. That's a good idea."

I shouldered the pack and then hesitated. He was standing waiting, his eyes closed, like a tired, patient horse. I put my hands on his shoulders. "You've got to put everything into it now, partner. Everything you've got left. I'm going to be with you every step of the way, but I can't get you there alone. Do you under-stand?"

172

He nodded. "Yeah. We're partners."
"Okay," I said. "Here we go."

I guess I'd never seen anybody do anything really brave. Not in real life. But nothing I'd ever seen on TV or read about or ever imagined could equal what Randy did to himself that afternoon. He marched, wobbling and stumbling but always keeping his feet, as I cleared the path ahead. We made it around the eastern curve of Black Dan, and then cut overland to the shore of Big Carry. Only then did I let him lie down for a few minutes.

By that time, I wasn't doing so hot myself. Maybe it was the hunger, or maybe the duck and beaver shit in the water, but I was feeling like hell, my stomach knotting with cramps and my skin oozing clammy sweat. And I wasn't thinking worth a damn. All the way from Black Dan, I'd held on to the hope that we'd spot a fisherman or a canoeing party on Big Carry, but I didn't even think to look until I was kneeling on the shore filling the canteen. For a second, my heart leaped into my throat, and I jumped to my feet to start waving and yelling at the boat far out in the middle of the lake. But then I saw that it was only a big, flat boulder with half a dozen ducks waddling about on the top, and I dropped my arms to my sides, my shout drifting off into the gray mist hanging on gray water. As far as civilization went, we might as well have been five hundred miles farther north, where people had to fly in to fish the lakes.

Randy opened his eyes for a moment. "What?" he said.

"Nothing. Nothing at all. Come on, we've got to move." I went to help him up.

I'd considered turning west along the northern shore of Big Carry for one more try at getting to the logging road, but chances were that the big swamp extended well to the south of Black Dan, a huge blob of gooey land enveloping the western shores of both lakes. So I led him to the east. We had maybe two hours of light and another half hour of twilight left. If we could get to the river on the south side of Big Carry by sunset, we might just be able to get within sight of Cant Hook by dark.

The shoreline of Big Carry hooked north around a bay that I'd failed to draw in on my mental map, and we lost the better part of an hour getting around it before we were going south again. Randy stumbled every few paces, righting his balance with a grunt each time. When he fell the first couple of times, I managed to help him up, but I was woozy and having trouble keeping my own balance. He wasn't talking at all any-more, and his eyes no longer seemed to focus, but he kept coming on behind. God, he was tough. Tougher than anybody I'd ever known. And I wasn't going to let him die.

God knows what those poisons were doing to his brain, but mine had kind of gone off on its own, digging up crazy stuff while my body kept moving without direction. I remembered Nicki, Bob's cocker spaniel, who'd died when I was still little. How come we'd never had another dog? I liked dogs. Maybe I'd get a big mean one and train it to keep the twins in line. How the hell old were they now? Eight? Nine? No, they were ten. I remembered that. Yeah, fourth grade. I remembered fourth grade. I'd had a crush on a girl named Linda. No, that was fifth grade. Or maybe sixth. What had ever happened to her, anyway? Come to think of it, what had happened to half the kids I'd known back then? I couldn't remember. And Sonia. What had happened to her? Nothing that I could think of, but somehow she seemed just as unreal as Linda. Everybody in the world seemed unreal. Everybody except me and Randy. We were all that were left.

Somewhere in all the crazy stuff jouncing around in my brain, I remembered a saying from a book I'd read in grade school about the French Foreign Legion: "A legionnaire can always march one more step." I tried to concentrate on that, promising myself that I'd take a rest after another twenty steps, and then not stopping but starting to count again every time I hit that twenty, because I, too, could always march one more step.

Randy stumbled and fell. He tried to get up, but couldn't. He'd spent everything he had. I tried to help him up, but I wasn't strong enough anymore. I slumped down beside him, worked the straps of the pack off my shoulders, and lay back against it. I wanted to close my eyes, to say to hell with it, but knew I couldn't. I struggled to my feet, reached down, and pulled him up. "Put your arm around me, partner. We'll do this yet." We left the pack behind and started off, wobbling along like a pair of drunks.

Ahead the shore rose sharply before leveling off along a low ridge that dropped back to lake level a few hundred yards to the south. No way could we make the climb, so we cut off on a deer path skirting the back side of the ridge. And there, just beyond a little clearing shadowed by thick cedars, we hit swamp again, and I had to let him down because we were finished and I knew it, knew it just as surely as if there'd been a big sign nailed to a tree at the edge of the swamp: "No way, Mark. No way, Randy. No way, José. You guys are screwed."

I leaned against a tree, the cramps twisting my guts, but afraid that I'd never get up if I flopped down beside Randy. I tried to tell myself that we'd have one last chance in the morning, but I didn't believe it. I pressed my forehead against the bark, trying to concentrate. It was going to get cold, and we needed a fire. And the pack. I couldn't do anything about the acids poisoning his system, but if I could keep him warm, he might be okay until morning.

I knelt beside him, rubbed a few drops of mosquito dope on his exposed skin, and then checked the tin of butterscotch candies in his pocket. Empty. He'd eaten or spilled the last of them somewhere back on that endless trail we'd traveled since morning. I helped him sit up against a big cedar and held the canteen to his parched lips. He managed to swallow a little, but most of the water ran down his chin. "Randy," I said, "I've got to go back for the pack. It's getting colder, and we can't sleep out here without something to cover us." He grunted, but I doubted if he understood. "Just stay here," I said. "I'm coming right back. We'll build a fire and get warm. Okay?" He didn't respond.

I hesitated a moment, wondering if I should hog-tie his feet with the piece of rope from around my waist.

But that might freak him out, and how far could he go if he tried? "I'll be back. Just hang tight."

I set out back the way we'd come, my feet weighing thirty pounds each. But it was already growing dark, and I kept lifting them up and laying them down like those legionnaires in the book I'd read, when all my dreams of doing brave things someday had seemed fairy-tale easy, not a matter of dying or not dying where nobody would find the bodies for days or weeks or maybe forever.

I reached the pack, got it on my shoulders on the second attempt, and trudged back down the trail. By the time I got near the swamp, all the trees had begun to look the same in the dusk, and for a minute I had the terrible feeling that I'd never find the little clearing where Randy lay by the big cedar. But just when I was about to panic, I stumbled into it and found him curled up where I'd left him. I dropped the pack and checked his breathing. He seemed okay. Or as okay as he'd been when I left. Don't sit down, I told myself. Don't even think about it. Now make the fire you promised him.

I gathered moss and enough twigs and sticks to get a fire going. Once I had some firelight, I'd find enough bigger stuff to get us through the night. I piled moss and a handful of twigs in a mound. My hands shook, and I had to concentrate everything I had to strike a match. The match flared up and blew out before I could cup my hands around it. I cursed and forced myself to go slow. The second match broke, its tip flicking like a firefly into the gloom. Last goddamn match. God, do we have to take everything to the absolute limit? I bit my lip hard, willing my hands steady, and struck it. The match spat fire, and I cupped it until it was going well before easing it under the tinder. Smoke curled up through the moss, followed by a thin yellow flame. I bent, blowing carefully as the flame hesitated and then began lapping at the twigs. The first two or three ignited slowly, almost painfully, and then suddenly they all flared up and I had to move quickly to add more before they burned out. I kept blowing, coaxing the flames to try bigger and bigger sticks as my back ached and the fire singed my eyebrows. Finally, I was able to sit back as the fire started crackling and the sparks rose into the dark where the dim outline of spruce and cedar tops hemmed in the window of sky. Thank you, God of Boy Scouting.

I spread out the sleeping bag a few feet from the fire and managed to roll Randy into it. Then I gathered three armloads of sticks and dragged a couple of small dead trees within reach. Only then did I let myself sit down at last, my back against the big cedar and a poncho wrapped around my shoulders. In a few minutes, I'd rig a lean-to in case it rained, but now I needed to relax for a couple of minutes. Just a few minutes to rest my eyes . . .

I awoke to the sound of thunder and the first twitch of wind scattering sparks from the dying fire. Oh, Lord. I tried to stand, but pain shot up my legs from my blistered feet. I gritted my teeth and forced them to take the weight. I threw an armful of sticks on the fire and blew like hell on the coals until the fire sprang up again. Then I hobbled over to the pack for the other poncho and the rope.

How I didn't cut a finger off, I'll never know. It was like I was caught in a dream, as my fingers cut the lengths of rope and threaded them through the grommet holes in the corners of the ponchos by the light of the fire and the first flickers of lightning through the trees. I was talking to myself, the sound of my voice strange in my ears. I remember thanking Dad for buying us good ponchos and for ordering me to read the instructions on the back of the package that showed how two ponchos could be made into a lean-to. I kept talking all the time it took me to get the ponchos lashed together, the corners on one side tied to a pair of trees, and the other side staked down with a couple of sticks — talking not because I was delirious or even that crazy yet, but because I needed the sound of my own voice in those few minutes before the storm.

I could hear the wind driving the rain across the lake. I didn't try to rouse Randy, just grabbed the head of the bag and dragged him under the lean-to. The trees bent and the lean-to quaked with the wind. I crawled out, got the stakes reset, and slid in again. It started raining then, cold and steady — a rain for the end of summer, for the end of warm green and sky blue and canoeing in the North. Rivulets ran down the sides of the lean-to and dripped through the seam where I'd knotted the ponchos together. I wrestled Randy as far to the dry side as I could, and sat shivering beside him.

Outside, the rain beat down the fire until only coals

hissed and then even their faint glow disappeared. I unzipped the sleeping bag and pressed in beside Randy. He felt cold, and I hugged him to me to give him what warmth I could. He groaned, and I hushed him, telling him that everything was okay, although I knew he wouldn't hear me now, and knowing that it wasn't.

We lay there as the thunder growled and the gray lightning lit the woods in black shadows and monstrous forms too uncaring to bother finishing off a couple of city boys who had done a pretty good job of that by themselves. I bit my lip hard. God, don't let Randy die tonight. Don't let me die.

CHAPTER TEN

I dozed, and when the storm finally blew over, slept. I dreamed then of bog, dark water, and shifting shadows beyond a small dry island where I lay beneath a tree so huge and so old it seemed of a species extinct since the Ice Age. Voices eddied in the shadows, and although I knew that I should recognize them, I couldn't match them with faces nor understand the language they spoke. And when they gathered and came closer, I cried out, half in terror, half in hope, and woke myself to the slow dripping of the trees and the damp wind blowing across a lake whose name I could not recall, nor cared for a minute to remember.

Randy groaned, tried to roll over, and then lay quiet again. I slid from the sleeping bag, tucked it around him, and crawled out of the lean-to. I hobbled a few steps away and took a whiz, feeling hollow clear through, the stomach cramps of the day before blessedly gone but replaced by a trembling emptiness. I stared at the patch of sky above the treetops, trying to decide if dawn was on its way or if the vaguely lighter dark was only the reflection of starlight penetrating the overcast.

I crept back inside and lay on the damp earth beside Randy. You need sleep, I told myself, and closed my eyes. But there was no more sleep in me. Instead, all my fears welled up. For a few minutes, I let them wash over me, and then tried to get hold of the simple truth that didn't need any added imagining to be terrible enough on its own: I was going to have to leave Randy and try to get out on my own. He wasn't strong enough to walk, and I wasn't strong enough to carry him. There was just no other choice.

When it was light enough to see, I crawled out and made my way through the trees to the back side of the low ridge blocking us from a view of the lake. I climbed up the wet slope, grabbing on to brush and stones to keep my balance. A raven swept low over the trees for a look at me, rising on tattered black wings with a squawk of disgust. Not quite dead yet, you bastard, I thought.

I stood on the crest in the damp breeze off the lake, the sight of the flat boulder that looked almost like a boat making me catch my breath for an instant before I recognized it again. In this whole damned country wasn't there a single fisherman with enough energy to get his ass onto something smaller than Cant Hook? Apparently not.

I studied the ground to the east, searching for a way through the swamp. I could barely make out the green ponchos of the lean-to through the trees. Cripes, I'd camouflaged us, not that anybody would be looking for us from the air yet. Not for another two or three days at least, and that would be far too late.

East and south of our campsite, the land fell away into a swamp of stunted spruce trees and mossy bog that stretched far beyond the curve of the shoreline — a land of muskrats and beaver, hawks and snakes, where no human being would ever walk in summer. I'd have to try the western side of Big Carry where there might or might not be a way through to the south and the logging road.

The wind from the west seemed colder then, colder than on the day we'd crossed Cant Hook fighting the big wind born over mountain snow and I'd dropped my compass into water as green and cold as melting ice. And even though the sun was rising clear, climbing over the trees and the last of the rain clouds scudding low on the eastern horizon, I had the sense of coming change, of the coming of the killing cold, when only those creatures adapted to this country or strong enough to get out would survive, while everything else died, food for the ravens, the foxes, and the scavenger bears in that brief autumn of dying before snow covered scattered bones.

Well, I wasn't ready to give up just yet. And it occurred to me in a sudden flash that I'd never been so free as I was at that exact moment. Dad, Bob, Uncle Jerry, or Pete might have known better what to do. But that didn't make any difference, because none of them were here to do it. I was, and whatever I did would be the best I could do. And if I died in the doing of it, died trying to save the one person who really made a goddamn difference to me anymore . . . Well, then for the first time in a long time, I wouldn't have anything to be ashamed of.

I took off my sweatshirt and climbed as high as I could into the tallest pine on the ridge. I tied a sleeve around a branch and left it flopping blue against the green. If people ever asked me for advice on traveling in the North, I'd tell them to wear nothing but fluorescent orange so the search parties could find them before it was too late — or at least spot their bodies in the spring. I made it back to earth in more or less one piece, leaving only a few shreds of skin on the bark, took one last look over the lake, and went to say good-bye to Randy.

I shook him gently a couple of times, but he was beyond waking now. So I zipped the bag up to his neck, placed the canteen within his reach, and spread the last of the mosquito dope on his damp hair and cheeks. "Partner, I'm going now. I don't know if you can hear me, but I'll be back with help. I promise. So you just lie here and sleep for a while." My voice caught, and I had to stifle a sob. "But don't give up. Because, goddamn it, we're partners, and we're not supposed to do anything unless we agree. And I don't agree to you dying. Not unless I get to go, too." I wiped my eyes. "So you just hold on, and I'll be back in a little while." I bent over, kissed his damp forehead, and then started north without looking back.

I passed the spot where I'd temporarily abandoned the pack to help Randy along, crossed our tracks south from Black Dan, and headed west along the north shore of Big Carry. At the channel between the lakes, I took off my boots, socks, and jeans and waded into the water in my shirt and underwear. I dressed on the far side, shivering in the breeze, and then pushed on to where the shoreline started to curve south. And, as I'd feared, I ran into the big swamp extending south from the western side of Black Dan.

Or at least I thought it was the same swamp, but after probing along its edges for a ways, I wasn't so sure. I checked the compass again, surprised to find that I'd managed to work myself farther west than I'd thought possible. Maybe this was a different swamp. And if that was true, then I might be moving into a gap between the two. I closed my eyes and tried to picture the thin dotted track of the logging road. Maybe I'd imagined it all along. But if my memory of the map was accurate, then the logging road had to lie not more than a mile to the southwest. If I could edge around the swamp without going too far west, I'd hit it. And, hell, I could be at the resort in a couple of hours. I opened my eyes, feeling adrenaline surging through my veins. I was right. My head knew it and my shriveling gut knew it. I studied the compass again and then set off in earnest.

The alley between the two swamps led me almost due west through thick brush. Tough going, but dry. Every two hundred paces, I'd probe south, feeling for the western edge of the swamp. But the swamp was still there, blocking my way. Then suddenly there was no more alley, just swamp to my left, to my right, and dead ahead. I couldn't believe it. I wouldn't believe it. I checked the compass, chose a bearing that felt right, rolled up my pant legs, and went in. If the legionnaires could do it in the desert, then goddamn it, I could do it in the swamp. One step, followed by one more step, and sooner or later I'd break through. I'd find that logging road. I'd find the resort. I would keep my promise to Randy.

I went into muck up to my ankles, then to my knees. I fought through to a mound of swamp grass, teetered on top, gauged my distance to a lump of moss, and leaped. I made it, my momentum throwing me forward, but there was another lump two yards farther on and I leaped again. I had this sudden, disembodied picture of myself, leaping from lump to lump, as if I were watching myself in a video game — one of the antic Italian plumbers leaping from toadstool to toadstool on the way to rescuing the princess. Shit, I couldn't even remember the name of the game, although I'd played it a thousand times. And I was making it work, running up the points and the distance, even while I knew it couldn't possibly last. Not for long, not even . . . I landed on the edge of a lump, it tilted, and I went off the side, arms flapping for balance, and splashed face-first into the muck. I tried to push myself up, but my hands felt no bottom, just sucking ooze. I slithered like a snake to the next ball of swamp grass, dragged myself up, teetered, gauging my distance, and leaped. But it was no good. The last of the big lumps of moss were behind me now, and my foot drove the next one straight down into mire. I plunged on, trying to run, as if speed alone could keep me from sinking in. And for maybe fifty feet, flat-out effort carried me, but then my right leg went in all the way to the thigh and I sprawled on my face.

I lay there, my cheek resting in the slime, as the mosquitoes and the blackflies swarmed thick around me, trying to penetrate the coating of mud on my body. They settled for trying to bore through the back of my shirt. I no longer cared. I was finished, and they might as well have some use of my carcass before it sank out of sight in the swamp.

I think I actually closed my eyes then, too exhausted to move or to cry. But the sharp point of one corner of the compass bit into my chest, and I pushed myself up an inch, and then another, until I was on my hands and knees. After that, I decided I'd try crawling a little way, and when that got tiresome, I struggled to my feet again. I stood there, rocking on wobbly legs, for I don't know how long before I got the compass from under my shirt, wiped the mud from the dial, and got my bearings again. I took a deep breath, waved away the blackflies trying to eat my eyeballs, and started back the way I'd come. The swamp sucked at my feet, as if it were trying to pull me down into the rotting vegetation of centuries, where I, like any other insignificant creature, would become part of the fossilizing goo of forever. But I wasn't quite ready for that, either.

For the next couple of hours, as I made my way out of the swamp and back along the blind alley to the lake, I didn't think a lot. Maybe not at all. I was beyond being discouraged or miserable or hungry or even tired. I'd been all those things, but they no longer mattered. I just moved because that was the last command my brain had given my legs. I wasn't even sure where I was going anymore. For a while, I had the picture in my head of making it back to the lean-to, where I could lie down next to Randy and wait for death: the Big D of all Big D's. But the picture faded away, too difficult, too unreal to hold on to.

I came out of the woods onto the shore of the lake with the sun already halfway down toward the western horizon. I rested beside the channel connecting Black Dan and Big Carry. I could just make out the narrow gap in the trees on the south side of the lake — the last river on the way home.

After a while, I went to the water's edge and washed some of the mud off my face and hands. I gazed at the sun, trying to judge the daylight left, and then stared across the lake. The distance wasn't huge, not as far as I'd had to swim after the canoe when it'd drifted away at the portage to Talking Bird, but I'd been in a lot better shape then. Still, it seemed the only choice left.

I stripped to my underwear and T-shirt, knotted the laces of my boots together, and shoved my socks down as far as I could into the toes. I remembered how a lifeguard had shown us a weird lifesaving technique when I was in Boy Scouts. He'd jumped into the pool wearing a pair of loose-fitting jeans and gone underwater to strip them off. Back on the surface, he'd tied the cuffs, zipped the fly, and swung them over his head to partially inflate the legs. Then he'd gone underwater again, blown air up into them, and, presto, produced an improbable set of water wings. Could I do that? I took a fearful look at the sun sliding toward the trees, knotted the cuffs of my jeans, and waded into the water to give it a try.

Cold? You wouldn't believe how cold. My balls and my richard pulled up tight, trying to crawl inside my abdomen. I stood in the water up to my waist, shivering and trying to get the stupid jeans to inflate. No luck at all, and my legs were already losing feeling when I floundered out. I dried myself with my shirt, trying to massage some feeling back into my legs. Then I tossed it beside my soaked jeans, slung my boots around my neck, and took a final look across the lake. A little more than halfway, I'd be able to rest on the big, flat boulder that looked like a boat. Make it that far without drowning, and you'll be all right, I told myself.

I took a running start, splashing in until the bottom went out from under me, and dove. With every stroke, the boots slapped against my shoulders, their drag in the water slowing me. Maybe a third of the way to the rock, I floated on my back to catch my breath. If I'd put more into swimming classes, I might have known some less exhausting stroke, but I could only do an overhand crawl and an awkward backstroke. Too late to worry about that now. I swung the boots around so they bounced against my back, but the laces across my throat choked me. Treading water, I tried slinging them over my left shoulder, then tried them across my chest again. No damned good. I threw them as far as I could toward the boulder, swam to them, and pitched them forward again.

On a warm day in warm water, I might have managed to save my boots that way. But by the time I was two thirds of the way to the rock, I was in big trouble. My left thigh and foot were cramping, and my arms weighed a thousand pounds each. I swam to the boots once more, missed the grab with a splash that sent them floating two yards to my right, and left them behind.

I was barely keeping my chin above water by the time I reached the boulder. My numb fingers slipped off the scaly surface, and I fell back into the water. If I didn't make it this time, I wouldn't make it at all. I threw myself forward, managed to get both hands on top, and flopped over like an exhausted walrus.

I lay there gasping on the warm rock, not minding that countless generations of ducks had used it as a rest stop and left the entire surface encrusted with duck shit. After the freezing water, even the breeze seemed warm as it dried me. A couple of times, vague orders to sit up drifted from somewhere deep in my brain, but my eyes closed anyway. I dozed, coming awake to the sound of a nearby splash. I opened my eyes to see a loon a dozen feet away, a small fish in its beak. The loon stared at me, its red eyes neither surprised nor curious. It shook the fish, lifted its beak, and swallowed it down. Then it let out its cry, the weird shivering note without a name that raised the hair on the back of my neck every time I heard it, because it always told me that up here nothing cared a damn if you lived or died. The loon stared at me again and then dove, a black flash disappearing into the watery shadows of that other world. I looked at the sun, saw its lower edge already brushing the trees, and wrenched myself upright.

I massaged my legs, trying to get the muscles loose.

Better than halfway there and no boots to worry about. Nothing except getting back in the water. I balanced on the edge of the boulder, took a deep breath, and dove, wondering only when I was in midair if there was a rock waiting just below the surface to break my neck. I hit the water, the shock of the cold going clear through me, and came to the surface stroking for the shore. It was immeasurably far, and my arms and legs were impossibly heavy. But somehow the spruce along the shore got bigger through my blurred vision, and I kept reaching out and pulling back against the water, kept kicking against it, although it felt like I was swimming in Jell-O. My vision tunneled down to a single tree, and the rest of my brain started spinning off crazy pictures that were gone as soon as they formed, leaving no memory except for a jumble of shapes and colors. The tunnel contracted to the size of a keyhole as the shapes and colors blurred into one another and the sensation of movement faded. And just when it hardly seemed worth the effort to lift my arms or kick my legs another time, I had a vague sense of rock beneath my feet — a feeling so faint that I almost decided to give up anyway. But my arms reached out a last couple of times and I had solid bottom under my feet. I staggered forward, fell, and crawled the last couple of yards out of the water and onto the beautiful grass beneath the trees.

I'm not sure how long I lay there, but the shadows were long and the sun well down into the trees by the time I finally managed to make it to my feet. I limped along the narrow beach to where the river disappeared into the trees on its way to Cant Hook. I'd pictured the river a thousand times on the map in my head. It ran almost straight down from Big Carry, and when I'd had boots, I'd imagined walking along its edge to the landing at the top of the short portage trail around the class four rapids just above the outlet into Cant Hook. But I knew my feet couldn't take the bruising on the rocks. It would be faster and easier to float as far as the portage trail.

The spring flood had tossed a splintered pine log on the shore. I pulled it free of the brush and shoved off into the current, one arm over the log, my feet kicking to keep me above the submerged rocks. Sonia, or whatever the hell her name was, would have gone apeshit with the excitement as we picked up speed, the water splashing over the broken nose of the log. I held on, trying to hear the sound of the big rapids ahead, my mind tensing for the moment I'd have to push clear to swim for the shore before I was swept into the rocks and chutes to be killed almost within sight of the big lake that had motorboats and people and a resort with cheeseburgers and IJ and help for the partner I'd left in the woods.

We swept down, the river seeming to tilt as the sound of heavy white water increased from a mutter to a steady rumble. The log pitched, tried to roll, and I kicked hard, my concentration momentarily lost in the effort of keeping it straight. That's what did me in, because when I got the log pointed downstream again, I saw the landing sweeping past on my left as the rumble ahead became a roar. A voltage surge the color of blue light flashed through my brain, and I pushed away from the log, kicking to get clear of its weight and splintered spines. It dropped over the ledge ahead of me, a ledge with a voice like Niagara. Or so it seemed to me as I got one brief look down before I tumbled over the falls, my howl lost in the thunder filling the world.

I hit and a gigantic hand pulled me deep, tumbled me like it was juggling a ball, then hurled me back toward the surface. I broke into air and light, but the deluge over the falls hammered me deep again, spun me, and slammed me against something hard and black and unforgiving. And then I rolled away in the river, everything I'd ever known, ever been, ever might have been, sucked up into a tiny ball far down at the center of a pain that swallowed me in a numbing dark.

I rolled in that darkness that was the river and not the river but something that I could no more name than I could recall who I'd been before the river had crushed me and left me rolling in darkness. And when my body scraped on the gray shale along the shore of Cant Hook, I did not know if I was dying or already dead, so I lay there, the water washing against me so that my body rocked with it like I was rocking in a cradle somewhere before memory had recorded anything but rocking and warmth. And if it hadn't been for the wind coming with nightfall to stir the trees along the beach, I might have lain there forever, but the wind brought back the sense of cold, a cold that focused the pain in my left shoulder and set the rest of me shivering in the rocking cradle of water on shale.

I don't remember getting to my feet and starting down the beach, but the movement shot pain from my shoulder down my left arm to the tips of my fingers.

I caught the wrist in my right hand and hugged it to my stomach. Somewhere in the distance, I heard my voice whining, talking disconnectedly in a language no more understandable than the voices in the dream that had wakened me in the darkness of dripping trees incalculable hours before.

Somewhere in the darkness and the cold, as the pain throbbed in my shoulder and the shale gouged at my feet, I guess I lost it completely, because a lot of what I saw and heard didn't make any sense later. On the lake, loons called, and it seemed for a while that I could understand what they were saying about fish and night and diving in cold, dark water. I think I tried calling to them, tried to ask them to guide me to where it was warm. But they took no notice of me, only cried to each other of the joy of night fishing.

Once I was sure that I saw a campfire with a man, a woman, and a child beside it. The man stood, the feathers and beads on his buckskins rustling. He stared at me, his face expressionless, his eyes pools of darkness. I tried to speak, tried to tell him that I was sorry for what white men had done to his race. But that I hadn't come to steal anything or to harm anyone. That I was just a stupid city kid lost in the wilderness. And if he could just help me this once . . . But before I could get any words out, he turned and spoke to the woman and the child at the fire and the three of them faded into the shadows beyond its light. And then it too faded and I fell and lay on the shale for a long time crying.

I think nothing more than the fear of dying alone made me get up, but when I stumbled on, I felt Randy beside me. Somehow he must have gotten his shot of IJ, and now he was well again and I was the sick one. I started to ask him if I could sit down to rest while he went for help, but then he wasn't there anymore and I knew that he must have died where I'd abandoned him near the shore of the lake whose name I had forgotten.

After that, I don't remember much except the northern lights playing over the trees — a jagged curtain of green, red, and yellow shafts leaping, blending, fading, and then leaping again. Somewhere in that time, I stopped caring about the pain or the cold or Randy lying dead with the fire of the aurora dancing in his upturned eyes. But my feet kept moving anyway. And at last, so small that I wasn't sure for a long time it was there at all, I saw a single electric light shining warm across the water.

I don't know how many times I lost sight of that light, or how many times I doubted that it was there at all. But my legs kept moving, and I found it again and then again and finally it broke into two lights and then three and I picked out the glow of windows in the darkness and the vague outline of buildings. I stumbled past boats rocking against a long dock reaching out into the lake, felt grass, then the sand of a driveway, and then grass again. My legs gave out, and I fell to my knees at the edge of the lawn. I knelt there, too tired to lie down or to call out from the darkness to the light.

A neon beer sign hung over the porch of the resort's tavern, and it struck me how pretty the colors were — tubes of liquid light swirling in fanciful letters like the track of a glowing pencil. I heard the murmur of talk and laughter beyond the door. Somebody told a joke, his low voice holding the bar's attention, and then I thought I heard my dad's booming laughter among the others. And I would have crawled toward it, but I couldn't because of my bad shoulder, so I rose again and staggered toward the door.

I tripped on the top step of the porch and sat down hard, leaning against the wall beside the door. Slowly, I laid my left arm in my lap, the pain in my shoulder a distant thing now, lifted my fist, and laid it hard — once, twice, three times — against the door. And, after I'd done that, I let my hand fall beside the other in my lap and closed my eyes, letting the easy darkness that I'd carried with me for so long have me at last.

CHAPTER ELEVEN

I came to lying on a pool table, my dad's face swimming above me. I smiled at him. He said something, but sleep seemed easier than trying to understand and I closed my eyes. "Mark! Don't fall asleep. Can you hear me?"

I looked at him again and grinned. "Sure, Dad. How you been?" I giggled.

"Give him some brandy," a strange voice suggested.

Somebody else snapped, "Don't be a goddamn fool, Billy. A drink would knock him out. There's another kid lost out there, and we've got to find out where he is."

Randy, I thought. I remembered him. But he'd died, hadn't he? God, maybe he hadn't! The thought jolted my brain to life, and I tried to sit up, but the pain in my shoulder sent the world spinning red and I lost track of everything but the pain. When I could concentrate again, Dad was trying to ask me things, but the words were coming too fast. "I gotta sit up," I croaked.

Dad laid a hand on my chest to keep me down and

then thought better of it. "Help me sit him up, Jerry," he said. I felt Uncle Jerry's hands under my damaged shoulder. I let out a whine of pain. "Steady, son," Dad said. "Just hold on."

They got me upright, and a big man with a short gray beard held a cup of something hot to my lips. I swallowed, tasting chocolate, and tried to take the cup in my good hand. "Easy," he said. "Let that go down first."

Uncle Jerry spoke, his voice vibrating with a panic just below the surface. "Ed, ask him again."

"I had to leave him," I said. "We wrecked the canoe and lost the medicine and he couldn't walk any farther, so I had to — " My voice started to break.

Dad held me. "Where is he, Mark? Is he still alive?"

"Yes, yes. He's by the lake just north of here. Big Carry. On the eastern side. I left him there this morning. I tied my sweatshirt — "

The big man with the gray beard was suddenly giving orders. "Pat, get hold of the ranger station. Tell Jim Maddox I want through the gate on the trail running up to the old CCC camp on Big Carry. Mitch, you got gas in your Power Wagon? Good. Frank, how about your bass boat? Got gas in the motor?" He went on giving orders, sending men running for chain saws, boats, and trucks, while I told Dad and Uncle Jerry what I could.

Finally, the big man turned back to us. He leaned in toward me, his face gigantic. "I'm Blitz Donner, and no goddamn jokes about reindeer, if you don't mind. I own this place." He reached out a huge hand and gently lifted my chin. He stared into my face, his small eyes, hidden in deep pouches, flaming blue. "And you are one hell of a tough kid to walk that beach with a broken collarbone and no boots. You can tell me that story later, but now you've got to tell me exactly where your buddy is. Then we'll get you off to a hospital."

"No! I'm coming along."

"Mark," Dad said, "you are all beat to hell."

"I don't care. Uncle Jerry, tell him I've got to come along."

Uncle Jerry hesitated and then leaned close, tears in his eyes. "Can you?"

"I promised him I'd be back."

Uncle Jerry looked at Dad. "Ed, it's your call."

Dad searched my face, his mouth tight. "All right. But we've got to get him taped up first."

"Good lad," Donner said, and then turned to shout over the din of men getting ready for the woods: "Who's got some clothes to fit this boy?"

A small, smiling old man with two missing fingers wrapped my arm tightly across my chest with Ace bandages. "Used to be a farmer. Good at doctoring all sorts of animals, and humans ain't much different. Done my share of dinging myself up, too. Broke my collarbone when I was a kid, and my daughter went and did the same thing when she was little. Runs that way in our family; every generation's just as clumsy as the one before. There, that'll hold the shoulder for a while. Feet are more of a problem, but we'll do our best. Your dad's getting some water and bandages." He looked toward the kitchen and then leaned in conspiratorially. "I still think that shot of brandy'd do you good. Want me to get you one?"

"No, that's okay."

"Well, when you get back, then. Just ask for Billy, and I'll get you one out the back door. Get you a couple. You earned it."

Dad came with the water, and together they worked on my feet. The pain shot up my legs like shards of broken glass, but I dozed off anyway. Dad lifted me to a sitting position. "Put your arm around my neck, son. Here we go." Together, he and Billy lifted me.

Outside, the yard shone with headlights, and I heard the growl of heavy engines. A dozen men were loading boats and trucks. Donner called to a tall, lean man standing by the open door of an old truck that looked like something from a World War II movie. "Mitch, you first. Surer than hell there's blowdown, and you've got the big winch. I'll come behind with one boat. Pat and Don, you follow with the other two. Mount up, guys."

Dad hoisted me into the front seat of Donner's truck, while Billy wedged himself into the narrow seat behind. I leaned back against Dad, feeling his warmth through his shirt. Donner revved the engine and we started off, the headlights of the trucks cutting through the dark tunnel of trees.

We rounded a bend, and I saw yellow lights revolving in the night. The ranger's truck stood at the turnoff to a narrow, overgrown track running north into the woods. Mitch's Power Wagon turned off the gravel, downshifting and growling ahead into the brush. Donner braked at the gate, calling out to the ranger. "Thanks for getting here fast, Jim. We'll have the kid out as soon as we can."

"I'm trying to get a medevac chopper in by eight. I'll land him on the field behind my place."

"We'll get there. Figure on the two kids and at least one of the dads."

"Gotcha. Good luck."

The truck bumped over ruts and potholes, brush scraping down its sides. We slewed through mud, Donner talking under his breath to the truck as he worked the gears. Ahead, Mitch's Power Wagon ground to a halt, and men scrambled out. "Blowdown," Donner said. "Come on, Ed. Billy, you stay with the boy." The trucks behind us stopped. I heard the sound of doors slamming as men jogged past us with chain saws and axes.

Billy climbed in beside me. In the headlights of the trucks, I saw Donner taking charge. Over the snarl of chain saws and the ratcheting of a winch unwinding, I heard his deep voice ordering some of the men to move ahead to clear the road farther on. Billy took a bottle out of a side pocket, and I caught the sharp smell of liquor as he took a drink. He gave a satisfied sigh and got comfortable with his back against the passenger door. "Lean on me, lad. Sounds like we'll be here a while." I let myself rest back against him, feeling the rough wool of his mackinaw against my skin and smelling the old man smell of chewing tobacco, brandy, and many years. It was somehow comforting, and I dozed again, listening to him humming softly.

I felt the truck lean as Donner climbed in. "Ed's gone

ahead with the crew. Looks like we've got a lot of blowdown. How's the boy?"

"We're doing just fine," Billy said. "Both having a little snooze while you guys work."

"Well, take it easy on the brandy, Billy. We need you sober. Or as sober as you ever get."

"Haven't had a drop, boss."

Donner snorted. "The hell." He dropped the truck into gear.

I dozed in and out after that, as the trucks bumped ahead, stopped, and after another delay, bumped on again. Finally, I heard Uncle Jerry, out of breath but in control, as he spoke to Donner through the open window. "We're clear for at least a quarter mile."

"Good. Quarter mile, and we're almost at the lake."

"Is Mark okay?"

"Yeah, he's doing fine. Get along ahead."

As we speeded up, the truck's bouncing lit up my shoulder with pain. Billy kept an arm around me. "Hang on, lad, almost there. You know, I wasn't much older than you when I helped clear this road back in the thirties so they could build the CCC camp on Big Carry."

"What's the CCC?" I said, not giving a damn, but wanting him to keep talking.

"Why, the Civilian Conservation Corps. Took kids out of the city and sent them into the woods to plant trees and clean up the mess left by the big logging companies. Paid a dollar a day, but that was big money back in the Depression. . . ." He rattled on, and I bit

202

my lip, trying not to cry out as the truck slammed over the bumps.

A red dawn was breaking on the flat surface of Big Carry when we finally made it into the clearing where the CCC camp had stood. Billy eyed the rising sun and smiled. "Red sky at morning, sailor take warning. We'll have another storm by afternoon."

"We'll worry about that then," Donner said. He swung the truck around, threw it into reverse, and backed the boat down to the shore. He climbed out, but Billy made me wait until Dad and the man I now identified as Mitch came to lift me out and carry me down to one of the boats.

Dad, Billy, Mitch, and Donner climbed in, followed by the driver, who yanked on the starting cord of the outboard motor. Nearly a dozen more men crowded into the other two boats. The boats rode low in the water, their motors laboring, as we started across the lake. Uncle Jerry rode in the bow of the boat to our left, leaning forward as if any second he'd jump out to try running across the water. "Dad, tell him to look for my sweatshirt up in the tree," I said.

"He remembers. Just relax, son."

It seemed to take forever to get there, the three boats cutting slow wakes across the lake as the reflection of the dawn faded to rose and then daylight blue. I looked back at the driver in the rear of the boat. Dark eyes in the broad Indian face met mine. I felt a shock of near recognition slap up against what I knew could not be true. For a long moment he watched me, his face impassive, and then he nodded solemnly, the faintest quirk of a smile twitching one corner of his mouth. Then he looked ahead over the water, paying me no more mind.

We passed the flat boulder that looked a little like a boat and on whose top I had lain gasping after nearly drowning on my swim across the lake. I searched the shoreline for the familiar rise of the ridge and the tall pine where I'd tied my sweatshirt. But the shoreline seemed more uniform now, the ridge hard to pick out, and the tree lost among the hundreds of others.

"There," Uncle Jerry shouted, and pointed. I followed the direction of his hand and just made out the faint blue flapping of a sleeve high in a tree. Before Uncle Jerry's boat even touched, he was out and reaching to help the next man.

We touched, and the driver killed the motor. Everybody jumped out except Billy and me. Dad turned. "Where, Mark? How far?"

I pointed. "Almost straight in. Maybe a hundred yards."

"Good. We'll find him." He hurried after the others.

Billy stretched, yawned, and winked at me. "Well, I guess I'd better get in on the excitement. You stay here and enjoy the peace and quiet. I'll be back." He climbed out and shambled up to where Donner had everyone spreading out in a search line.

I could have shown them exactly the spot where I'd left Randy. Damn it, I would show them. But they'd already disappeared into the woods by the time I could hobble up on the shore. I limped after them, trying to get my bearings. Nothing looked quite like

I remembered, and I had to fight down a twinge of panic. Damn it, this had to be the place. My sweatshirt was here and Randy had to be.

I moved from tree to tree for support, listening to the men moving ahead through the brush. For a moment, I thought they'd swung too far to the north and would miss him, but then somebody shouted, "I see him. He's over here under a big cedar." A moment later the same voice called, "He looks pretty rough, but he's breathing."

Uncle Jerry rushed past me, fumbling with a syringe and a bottle of insulin. I limped ahead as fast as I could. At the edge of the little clearing, I stopped, leaning against a tree. Half a dozen men were gathered around Randy. They'd torn away the lean-to and stripped off the sleeping bag, and now Uncle Jerry was leaning over him, unfastening his pants. He swabbed a spot on Randy's abdomen and poised the syringe, its needle flashing in a shaft of sunlight. Then it was in, and Uncle Jerry pushed the plunger home.

It was done, and I let myself slide slowly down the trunk of the tree and closed my eyes. I heard footsteps and Donner's soft laugh. "Well, he made it all the way back. You've got one hell of a boy there, Ed."

"I know it," Dad said, and I felt strong arms lift me.

CHAPTER
TWELVE

"I thought you'd be up and about by now, partner. You're not wimping out on me, are you?" Randy stood at the door of my hospital room in Ely, where they'd flown us from the ranger station.

I stretched in the coolness of clean sheets. "Yeah, I'm definitely taking the wimp route from now on. How're you doing?"

"Oh, pretty good." He gestured at his eyes, hidden behind dark glasses. "Vision's kind of fuzzy, and *the Mom* is taking me back to St. Louis so my regular doctor can check it out. I don't think it's any big deal. In a couple of days, everything will clear up. How's the shoulder?"

"Doesn't hurt at all now. Six weeks and it'll be as good as new. Feet might take longer."

"Yeah, my dad said they looked like hamburger by the time you got to the resort."

"Well, it was kind of hard going there at the end. . . . So, when'd your mom get here?"

"Yesterday afternoon. Did everything but bring the divorce papers with her. They had it out big time last

206

night, so I guess that's it for that. She's moving out with Marcia soon as I'm okay."

"I'm sorry."

He shrugged. "It's kind of a relief. About time everybody stopped lying and just got it done. Anyway, she's coming in to see you in a while. Thank you for saving my life and all that."

"Nobody saved anybody's life. We got in trouble together and we got out of it as well as we could together. You worked just as hard at staying alive as I did."

He shuffled, embarrassed. "Well, thanks, anyway. Some other guys would have given up on me."

"I don't think . . . Oh, hell. Okay, you're welcome. But tell your mom I'm asleep."

"Never work. You're on her schedule." He glanced at the clock in the hall. "Well, I'm supposed to see the doctor once more before we head out. Gonna stay with your mom in Minneapolis tonight."

"Just don't mess with my girl on your way through town."

"Wouldn't think of it. Well, we'll see you."

"Yeah. Keep in touch."

"Sure," he said.

"Hey," I called after him, "you still owe me about six cheeseburgers."

"Two. You need to lose some of that gut." And he was gone.

That night I had a fever and the next day a nifty infection in my right foot, which kept me in the hospital another three days. Mom insisted on coming to Ely, so Dad went back to Minneapolis to take care of the twins and to convert the den into a bedroom, since it'd be a while before I could climb stairs again.

I guessed that something was up when Mom pulled in at a rest area twenty miles from home to use the phone. When she got back in the van, I said, "Mom, they aren't planning anything embarrassing, are they?"

"Not a thing, dear." She smiled at me innocently. Oh, shit, I thought.

Sure enough, a welcoming party of about twenty of the neighbors started applauding when we turned into the driveway, while Dad and the twins stood proudly under a huge sign they'd hung from the garage door: WELCOME HOME, HERO.

"Mom," I said, "why'd you let — "

"Now be gracious, dear. A lot of people have put in a lot of effort to show how much they care."

I guess I pulled it off, blushing modestly and doing the ah-shucks-it-weren't-nothin' routine until they finally let me go inside to rest.

When everybody'd gone home, Mom came into my new bedroom. She adjusted the pillow behind my head and then handed me an envelope. "Your brother wrote. I think he's very proud of you, dear."

I stared at the envelope, with is official return address: *Robert O. Severson, Cadet Commander, Army ROTC Battalion* . . ."Thanks," I said.

"So is there anything you need before I go help your father clean up outside?"

"No, thanks, Mom. I just want to rest for a while."

When she'd left, I tore open the envelope to see what Bob the Nazi had to say.

Dear Mark,

Dad called me from the hospital in Ely and told me how courageous you were in saving Randy's life. You made him very proud. I told him that I'd known all along that you had guts and grit. You just kept it pretty well hidden for a while. Now, we can all be proud of you again.

All that said, I think it might be worth your time to think about some of the decisions that got you into trouble in the first place. For example, when Pete and I . . .

I let the letter drop onto the bedcovers and stared out the window at the sky graying with late-summer clouds. Rain tonight, I thought, and wondered if the same clouds were gathering over Talking Bird and Ax Handle and if any canoers were even now bending to their paddles to make it down from the lakes ahead of the cold rain and the coming of fall. Then very carefully, I folded Bob's letter into a paper airplane. And when I was sure that it was every bit as good a paper airplane as Bob or anyone else had ever folded, I sent it gliding across the room so that it smacked into the wall and dove nose-first into the wastebasket. I smiled. Bull's-eye.

When I called Sonia that night to tell her that I'd made it back alive, she wasn't exactly overwhelmed by the news. So I was prepared when she came by the house the next day sporting a guy's class ring on a chain around her neck. She gave me a peck on the cheek and then sat down and crossed her long, tanned legs. "Whose ring?" I asked.

She grinned, half embarrassed, half pleased with herself. "Rob Newton's. He's a lifeguard at the water park. I know you've seen him there."

"Probably, but I never knew any names."

"Well, he's tall and blond, and he's got a silver star earring."

"Charming," I said.

She ignored that. "You'd like him. He helped me get a job taking tickets. The next time you're out there, I'll introduce you. Bring a girl some Tuesday evening. That's when we use our passes to do some slides. We'll get you in free."

"Don't hold your breath, I plan to stay a long way from water for a while."

"Oh, poo," she said. "Water never hurt anybody."

So that was it for Sonia. And, surprisingly, I didn't much care. If she couldn't wait ten days, she wasn't worth crying about.

I spent the next couple of days trying to keep myself busy, but I couldn't find much to hold my interest. Finally, I bribed the twins into going to the attic for my paints. I didn't have any big plans. This was definitely not the start of a career, just something to pass the time. I tried something simple, just the boulder in the middle of Big Carry and the loon with the fish. It didn't work worth a damn. The truth was that I could splatter colors around with the best, but I couldn't draw worth a damn.

That evening I asked Dad if he could pick up a book on drawing for me. "Sure," he said. "I've got to run out on some errands after supper. I can stop by the bookstore then."

"No rush. It's no big deal."

He hesitated. "You know, I used to be a pretty fair hand at drawing. Maybe — "

"Yeah, I know you were, Dad. But I'd just like to work at it by myself for a while." He looked disappointed. "Maybe in a few days you could show me some stuff," I said.

I missed the first two weeks of school, and it was October before I could walk without a crutch or a cane. I got the bandages off my shoulder about the same time, and the doctor put me on a physical therapy program to get the strength back in my arm. By then, I'd lost ten pounds to add to the six or seven I'd lost on the trip — and that despite Mom cooking every one of my favorite suppers while I was laid up.

The story of the canoe trip was old news by the time I got back to school, but I still got more notice than I'd ever had before. And that was fun until I got sick of correcting all the wild versions of what was really a pretty simple story.

I had dates with two or three different girls over the next couple of months and enjoyed them, but after Sonia I was being cautious. Everything would work out, I figured. Meanwhile, I had to get caught up on about two-and-a-half years of school work. And my art, too, because it looked like I was hooked on more than just the colors now.

Randy and Uncle Jerry came up for Thanksgiving. Uncle Jerry left the next day to spend the weekend in Chicago with "a friend." Or, as Randy described her: "the bimbo from accounting."

We were sitting in the den, watching the Packers

beating on the Vikings. "You met her yet?" I asked. "Formally, I mean."

He laughed. "Oh, yeah. Actually, she's not too bad. Not a bimbo at all, really. I just wish to hell I hadn't seen 'em getting it on that time in Dad's office. Kind of gives one a lasting impression."

I grunted. "So how's your mom?"

"*The Mom* is fine. I had lunch at her place last Saturday. One of the partners from the firm *just happened* by to drop off some papers. That torqued her, because he hadn't called for an appointment first. This is not a spontaneous lady, believe me. But I figure she'll forgive him soon enough. I think he's the one she's been seeing all along. Everything adds up that way."

"Regular soap opera."

"Some of that, I guess. Did I tell you Marcia didn't move out after all?"

"No."

"Well, she and *the Mom* decided she'd be happier staying close to her friends."

"The ones who like your buns."

"Yeah, that bunch. Anyway, she's spending a lot of time at Mom's new place, but she's living with Dad and me. I like it that way. We have a lot of fun."

"That's good. Is your dad laying a lot of new rules on you?"

"Nah. He was headed that way, but we had a long talk. I told him that I'd learned a lot on the trip and that I'd never get my butt caught in a wringer like that again. So he backed off on the rules."

"So," I said, "no more canoe trips, huh?"

"Oh, I didn't say that. As a matter of fact . . ." He

pulled a map from a shirt pocket. "I've got next summer's route all planned out. Let me show you where we're going, partner."

He spread the map out on the coffee table, and I leaned forward to look. Deep down, in a still place that lay now just within my touching, a loon cried, its call echoing across far blue waters.

About the Author

Alden R. Carter is an award-winning author of fiction and nonfiction for young adults. Among his novels are *Sheila's Dying*, *Growing Season*, and *Wart, Son of Toad*, all American Library Association Best Books for Young Adults. In 1994, his novel *Up Country* was named one of the 100 Best Books of the Last 25 Years by the Young Adult Library Services Division of the ALA. His novel *Dancing on Dark Water*, named Best Children's Fiction Book of 1990 by the Society of Midland Authors under its original title, *RoboDad*, is now available as a Scholastic Point Paperback. His most recent novel is *Dogwolf*.

Mr. Carter lives in Marshfield, Wisconsin, with his wife, son, and daughter.